Other Titles by TW Brown

The DEAD Series:

DEAD: The Ugly Beginning
DEAD: Revelations
DEAD: Fortunes & Failures
DEAD: Winter
DEAD: Siege & Survival
DEAD: Confrontation
DEAD: Reborn
DEAD: Darkness Before Dawn
DEAD: Spring
DEAD: Reclamation
DEAD: Blood & Betrayal
DEAD: End (October 2015)

I0531542

DEAD Special Edition

DEAD: Perspectives Story (Vols. 1 & 2)
DEAD: Vignettes (Vols. 1 & 2)
DEAD: The Geeks (Vols. 1 & 2)

DEAD: Snapshot— {Insert Town Here}

*DEAD: Snapshot—***Portland, Oregon***
*DEAD: Snapshot—***Leeds, England** (August 2015)

Zomblog

Zomblog
Zomblog II
Zomblog: The Final Entry
Zomblog: Snoe
Zomblog: Snoe's War
Zomblog: Snoe's Journey

That Ghoul Ava

That Ghoul Ava: Her First Adventures
That Ghoul Ava & The Queen of the Zombies
That Ghoul Ava Kick Some Faerie A**
Next, on a very special That Ghoul Ava
That Ghoul Ava...on the Lam!

You can find my titles on Audio as well.

Audible.com

That Ghoul Ava
...on the Lam!

(Do you seriously read these and wonder if they matter to the story?)

TW Brown

https://www.facebook.com/pages/Author-TW-Brown

Portland, Oregon, USA

That Ghoul Ava...on the Lam!
©*2015 May December Publications LLC*

The split-tree logo is a registered trademark of May December Publications LLC.

This book is a work of fiction. Names, characters, businesses, organizations, places, events, and incidents either are the product of the author's imagination or are used fictitiously. Any resemblance to actual persons living, dead, or otherwise, events, or locales is entirely coincidental.

This book is protected under the copyright laws of the United States of America. Any reproduction or unauthorized use of the material or artwork contained herein is prohibited without the express written permission of the author or May December Publications LLC.

Printed in the U.S.A.

ISBN 978-1-940734-44-6

Printed in the United States of America.

Lam: *(lăm) v.—intransitive verb to escape or run away, especially from the law.*

This book is dedicated to Caroline.
She loved Ava enough to start a fan club.

A moment with the author…

I have been accused of being a sell-out. Now, before you ask who could hurl such an accusation, I will admit to that very thing right here in print. My *That Ghoul Ava* series is written with the hopes and dreams of commercial success attached. This book is far more "film friendly" than, say, my *DEAD* series. These books are written with a specific demographic in mind: Women. And for my male Ava fans, I love you guys as well, but the stats show more women read than men. (That would explain the over-abundance of bodice rippers out there.)

Maybe you already know this story, but when I started this series, I was writing that first short for one of my very first fans. I turned her Twitter handle into a story. It was a "thank you" note from me. However, a few people got their hands on it and said that I had something. I had enjoyed writing it so much that I decided to focus a NaNoWriMo event on it. And that was when Ava met *The Queen of the Zombies*. (Yep, that "The" is still capped!)

Afterwards, I went on a binge of reading some of the vast numbers of books under the "Urban Fantasy" heading. I was already reading Laurell K. Hamilton's *Anita Blake* series. I fell off when she turned it into soft core porn, but those first few books had some great horror elements. Then I found what I think must be considered a prototype for the genre: Kim Harrison's *The Hollows* series with Rachel Morgan.

I make no bones about how I have my hopes pinned to this book series going commercial, but that is why I need your help. You are my readers, and I value each and every one of you. I am hoping that you will tell your friends about "this great new series that you just HAVE to read!" As an Indie writer, my advertising budget consists of the time I spend to lay these requests at your feet. This is no less important than my request for reviews (which also drive sales).

I will continue to write this series for the next few years because I love Ava. I will continue to hope that some magic switch is thrown and other people find her as you have and enjoy her quirky humor. And seriously, that is the hardest part about writing Ava.

As a zombie author, I can just let the story come as it unfolds before me, but Ava has to have an end game for each book, and there has to be a few chuckle-worthy moments. Comedy being subjective, I can only hope that you get at least one snort or giggle from these books.

So, as I wrap up this rambling note to you with Christmas music blaring from my computer (Trans-Siberian Orchestra is shredding guitars in a cool rendition of *The Nutcracker Suite*), I just want to thank a few special people have already picked up the Ava banner and waved it proudly: Caroline Harmon, official president of the *That Ghoul Ava* fan club—you are awesome and I appreciate all that you do. I never thought I would have a fan club in any fashion attached to anything I wrote, so let me say thank you with all sincerity. Ramona Martine, the first person to have an Ava Halloween costume, all I can say is "Wow…just wow!" And to Pamela Lorence, you bring my story to life in my ears, and I don't think you will ever know how much I anticipate listening to your narration of the audio book version as I complete each *That Ghoul Ava* story.

"So…what do you little maniacs want to do first?
TW Brown
December 2014

Contents

1

Breaking the Law

Seriously, how do I get myself in these situations?

I guess that is what happens when you fight against your nature. As a ghoul, I am learning that my nature has a lot more to it than simply eating the dead. I never in my life thought that I would be the Supernatural equivalent of a mercenary or a bounty hunter. Hell, I can count the number of fights I have been in on one hand. Well, until I became a ghoul at least.

The last one was a catfight with this cocktail waitress named Cherry Ladd. Stupid name. How was I supposed to know it was her real one and not her made up "stripper" name? Some people get so touchy. I absolutely did *not* deserve to be slapped.

In the past three hours, I have been in five hand-to-hand fights. And they all ended in death. Not mine of course, or I would not be telling this little tale.

From the way these damn Templars are coming after me, you would think that I was the one who had killed all those children. The fact that this all started when Morgan sent me to investigate the recent disappearances of those missing kids allows me to have somebody to blame this on. Oh yeah, I'm totally blaming her.

I can hear footsteps coming. Taking a deep breath, I try to clear my mind and then let it wander so that the pain I am about to experience does not slow me from finishing my mission.

Crap.

My mind is falling back on that old and overused gimmick. Be prepared for a flashback that will actually bring you up to speed as to how I got here.

***

"This is a bad idea, Ava," Lisa insisted.

"Which is absolutely why I have to do it," I replied with a shrug.

Seriously, has she not been paying attention? None of my ideas ever start out as good ones. Heck, most don't end up that way either, but if you ask a hundred guys if they want to buy you a drink, you will eventually get one that will say yes. Actually, I usually didn't have to ask more than two or three before getting one to pony up. I so-o do not miss those parts of my old life.

"Morgan is on her way over to the house." Lisa grabbed my arm.

I must have twitched around the corners of my mouth, because when I looked down at that hand and then back at her, she let go and took a step back. I wish she would get it through her head that, Templar or not, I was not ever going to hurt her.

With a single leap. I was on the roof of the house. I had no trouble spotting my objective. I reached in my pocket and pulled out the sealed Tupperware container. Moving quick and quiet, I reached the chimney. A pleasant whiff of burning wood twisted in the single coil of smoke that was twirling and drifting sky-wards.

I peeled back the red lid and was quickly greeted by an acrid and bitter stench. Poop. A huge, steaming pile of Great Dane butt custard.

You see, I have a neighbor with a pair of big, lovable Great Danes. I do not blame the dogs one bit for their indiscretions. They have discovered a lovely yard where they can relieve themselves anytime they wish. The problem?

IT'S MY YARD!

Maybe I should back up the story and clarify a few things. Be patient with me…it has been a hectic time and a lot of bad things have happened in a short period of time.

***

The first time Nose Wart stepped in a pile, I learned a whole new string of curses. It didn't help that I laughed. Seriously, goblins are so nasty. I guess the whole scene just struck my funny bone. Here is this filthy goblin that makes it a habit of burrowing in Lisa's compost pile for an hour, popping up every so often with something goopy dripping from the corner of his mouth which he licks away with his huge cow-sized tongue before he thanks us for properly aging egg shells and melon rinds; and yet he complains about stepping in a pile of dog poop which, in my opinion, smells much the same as that compost pile.

This evening, just after sunset, we had walked outside to the back yard so he and the other goblins could do some rooting and rutting in that nasty dark box Aoife had helped build for our scraps or whatever they dump out there (yeah, I mean exactly what you think in regards to the rutting bit, and I refuse to say another word on the subject). Nose Wart emerges, rubbing his bulging belly. He was three steps from the composting pile when he froze and screamed in a way that brought on switch fingers, toes, and Sharkmouth in an instant.

"What vile intestine scrapings are these?" Nose Wart lifted his foot straight out in a pose that would make a yoga class instructor jealous.

It took me a second, but with my superior eyesight, I quickly identified the pile of Great Dane doo doo. Actually, I noticed seven. It was as if my yard had been turned into a dookie mine field.

I knew right away where these had originated and turned sharply to go and confront the neighbor. Nose Wart followed on my heels muttering a continuous sting of curses that actually started to make me have to suppress a giggle. I am not kidding; if you ever get a chance to hear a goblin swear, I dare you to keep a straight face.

Since it was still early in the evening, Lisa's paint job coupled with my dark glasses would keep my undeadness from being apparent to the humans next door. I actually was beginning to think I could get away with just the glasses, people are so politically correct these days that I believe folks would be afraid to mention my gray skin for fear of being called racist.

Anyway (I wish I sounded as cool saying that as Joel McHale), a few minutes later, I knocked on the neighbor's door. The man who answered was freakishly tall, and skinny to the point that he looked as if a stiff breeze could send him tumbling.

"Yes?" he said in a voice that was deeper than Bowzer's from Sha-Na-Na.

"Who is it, Richard?" a female huffed like she was at the last stretch of a hundred yard sprint. The sound of feet thundering up some stairs announced her presence.

It was almost funny in just how stereotypical this couple looked. She was short, and by short, I mean she is a bii-i-iig liar if her driver's license says she is five feet tall. In one hand, she held (no joke) a box of Twinkies. In the other she had a big glass of chocolate milk.

"I was just asking, Sugar Dumpling."

Yuck.

Richard turned to me and folded his arms across his chest. He was just about to open his mouth—I assume it was to ask me my name—when a monstrosity forced its head between the man and the partially open door. A huge head swung up at me and the mouth opened as a deep 'woof' came rumbling from the dog's throat.

"Greetings, I am Dredge, but the humans call me Rex."

I was struggling to keep Sharkmouth at bay from the initial fright, when I did a double-take. Cocking my head, I asked the massive hound, "Are you talking to me?"

"Down, boy, back in the house!" Richard commanded.

"Hmm, perhaps I will be enjoying a treat!"

Of course, all the human—err...I mean Richard—all he heard was another woofing bark and then there was a scrabble of claws on hardwood floor as the dog vanished down the stairs. Of course that would not have been possible if the enormous woman had not finally reached the landing.

I would have to explore why I apparently understood the massive hound later, but at the moment, I was holding a Dave's Killer Bread bread bag that was heavy with dog logs. Even after having squeezed the top shut and spinning it to seal it, the stench was gaggingly strong.

"Hi, I'm your neighbor, and I think your dogs have been using my yard as a toilet." No sense in beating around the bush, right?

"How do you know it is our dogs?" Sugar Dumpling huffed, golden cake crumbs flecking the edges of her mouth and flying through the air with each word.

"I could start with the sheer size and volume, but how about the fact that I don't own a dog and we have no neighbors within a few miles." That seemed like a perfectly reasonable reply.

"Wolves!" Sugar Dumpling shoved her husband aside and damn near filled the entire lower two-thirds of the doorframe.

At first I thought she was warning me. Seriously, the way she practically shouted it, I actually looked over my shoulder. Nose Wart and his little band of goblins were clustered together, but other than that, I didn't see, hear, or smell a thing.

"Excuse me?" I turned back to the woman.

"Coulda been wolves."

She plucked another poor defenseless Twinkie from the box and, with mad skill, she snapped the plastic open with index finger and thumb. One bite. No lie. She popped that whole golden snack cake into her mouth like it was nothing more than a vitamin pill.

"Umm, no." I leveled my gaze at the woman, fighting the desire to pull off my shades and give her the full on, black eyed glare. "It was your dogs. So all I am asking is that you keep them in your yard to do their business."

"Git your skinny ass offa my porch."

After that, a lot of very unpleasant words were exchanged. I was so proud of myself. No switchfingers or toes. I left them alive and well. And when I reached the end of the little walkway that led to their porch, I turned and sent that bag of dog poop flying at their closed door where it hit with a wet splat.

There was a second or two of silence…and then a rousing chorus of hoots and cheers erupted and broke the night's peace. I spun on Nose Wart and his gang.

"Hush!" I scolded. "Now get home before somebody sees you."

"Humans can't see us, Just Ava," Nose Wart scoffed. I really needed to correct him on my name. You would think that he might figure it out with being around so often when others talk to me.

I dismissed the comment and shooed them away with my hands. All the way home, I tried to think of something that I could do to Bean Pole and Sugar Dumpling. When I walked inside, Lisa was just getting off the phone. She looked like I had just walked in to catch her *en flagrante delicto*. I looked around and did not see a boy with his pants around his ankles trying to escape through a window. That left—

"Templar Business?" I said with as little emotion as I could manage. I could feel my finger tips and toes starting to tingle.

"Not every single call to me has to be from the Templars. I know other people."

I did not say a single word. I just folded my arms in front of me and dropped my chin so that my eyes peeked over my dark glasses. I heard a slight shuffle behind me as Nose Wart and the other goblins headed downstairs. They always vanished whenever I got even a little annoyed.

One time, I was watching *Wheel of Fortune* and the stupid lady kept buying vowels. Seriously, unless there is a rule stating that you must buy a certain amount to be able to win, I do not understand some of those people. I got annoyed, and all of a sudden, the entire pack ran downstairs. I did not see them again until the next day.

"Fine," Lisa muttered. "It was Race."

She could have said anything in the world after that and I would not have heard a single word. I have gotten better at controlling my mind wandering episodes when people talk except when I am being tortured. Then it becomes one of my secret ghoul powers to ignore pain. Who knew that ADD would be such a boon?

Race Mitchell is Lisa's handler. He is also in the upper chain of command with the Templars who, as it just so happens, are the group that tried to eradicate every ghoul from the face of the earth way back in the days of the Inquisition.

Race Mitchell is also super dreamy. He has that look about him that screams "Bad Ass!" Oh, and yes, his ass is super luscious, so that could actually be taken to mean more than one thing. He has eyes that cut into me and turn my bones to movie house popcorn butter. His arms are like iron constructs with steel cables for muscles. And his chest? You could use it as a movie screen if he wore a white tee-shirt. Almost perfectly jet black hair and a swarthy complexion made him into serious eye candy. Basically, he made Antonio Banderas look like Pee Wee Herman.

"He says that he might have something that can take you off the most wanted list, but until he can be sure, he wants you to stay low key." Lisa was heading into the kitchen.

I heard her rummage in the refrigerator, and that was when I realized that I had not eaten yet. I headed for the basement. It wasn't the awesome soundproof room that we had back in the other house. This place apparently used to be a huge former Christmas Tree farm that had been foreclosed back when the economy went so bad in 2006 or whenever that happened.

Unlike my state-of-the-art, all modern conveniences, and super nice house that I had been so proud of with its titanium, light proofing blinds, this place is…well…it's an old farm house with a big basement that has been permeated with the smells of all the Mason jars of pickles, strawberries in various forms, and whatever else these people used to can depending on the season. The walls are all floor-to-ceiling shelving where they stored their goods for decades. Basically, this place sucks. We bought it because it sits on eighty or so acres. Plenty of room for the jötunn.

I opened the chest freezer. Hmm, just one corpse left. I

would have to head out tomorrow and cruise downtown. It is really sad how many homeless just die and nobody notices. But, when life deals you lemons (or dead winos)…

"Evening, miss." Aoife shimmered and stepped out of the darkness.

That was another benefit of this place. I guess it sat on some sort of node that the faeries covet. When they link their sidhe to it, I guess it boosts the healing powers of the Godmother. (I can thank Blodwen for pointing it out.) This gave me something to offer Rain. Between that and promising her that all the faeries could do whatever it is that fairies do in the woods anytime they pleased, and that I would not re-open the place as a Christmas Tree farm, I was on good footing with the fey.

"I was just getting ready to eat," I told Aoife. Actually, it was more of a warning. She did not like to be around when I fed.

"Very well." Aoife scurried for the stairs. As she scampered up, she called over her shoulder, "Rain says that Morgan will be coming to see you soon."

I dismissed the comment and let Sharkmouth come. It was supper time! In a matter of just a few moments, I was sitting on the beanbag chair in the corner, rubbing my belly in contentment. There was this perfect moment of peace where I was able to shut out the voices in my head as well as those upstairs.

I should have known it was too good to last.

"I will pluck the eyes from their sockets and replace them with the testicles of a syphilitic goat!"

The tiny stomping feet of an angry goblin broke the spell and I sat up. I could see Nose Wart and his little brood pouring down the stairs in a rush. They only took a second to locate me and then it was like watching a swarm of locusts hone in on a fresh field of whatever it is that locusts like to eat.

"The human pigs have allowed those horse-dogs to leave their filthy droppings in our yard once again." Like a bull being taunted by a red cape, Nose Wart began pawing his feet on the rough and cracked concrete floor. It was not until the smell hit me that I realized he was wiping off the aforementioned filth on the floor of my basement.

"Did you track that into my house!" I gasped.

Just as he and the others goblins had been seething with a typical goblin display of bluster and anger only moments ago, they were all suddenly groveling at my feet like I had threatened to slice them open and eat their entrails. Perhaps later, I could examine what would possess my mind to use that particular analogy.

"Forgive! Mercy!"

A chorus of cries and shrieks came in a flood and I heard the sounds of feet coming at a run on the hardwood floor over my head. I knew it was Lisa and that was confirmed when she leapt down the stairs, hands on a pair of weapons swinging from her hips that I did not recall seeing when I had returned home just a little while ago.

"Easy there, Samurai," I warned as I held my hands up to stop Lisa's charge. "It was just the goblins. They stepped in some more of our neighbors' dogs' little turd land mines. Well, they aren't little, but you get my point."

I saw Lisa relax. Then she looked down at her stocking feet. It was like seeing a time lapse of a blooming flower, only in reverse. She lifted one foot and then the other, examining what was smeared and now fairly well ground in to her formerly pretty, pink ankle socks.

"Uh-huh," I nodded. "This calls for drastic measures."

Being careful not to step in the little smears, splatters, and dirty dollops of doody, I made my way to the steps. I was halfway up when it dawned on me that Nose Wart and the others were still huddled in a clump as they awaited certain death at the claws and teeth of the resident ghoul.

"Nose Wart!" I did my best to make my voice sound sweet and motherly. "You and the others get all of this mess cleaned up. I do not want to see or smell any evidence when I get back."

I heard a chorus of submissive "Yes, ma'am!" and "Right away, ma'am!" fade as I ducked into the kitchen and searched frantically for something. My eyes lit on an old Tupperware container that was stained an ugly orange from some pasta sauce or other that had probably sat in it until it became hairy and put up a fight when it came time to be thrown out. The red lid that fit it was in the strainer as well, and I grabbed them up as I made for the door, slipping into my all-black coat that goes down to my shins. I always feel like Neo from *The Matrix* when I wear it.

"Where are you going?" I could hear Lisa yelling as the door slammed shut. "Race said that you need to lay low!"

Good thing about my supercharged senses, it was easy to see as well as smell the new and offending piles. Using the plastic lid and being very careful not to get any of the offensive matter in the edges, I flicked the one that was still in pristine coils into the container as well as scraping up as much of the stepped in smooshed pile that Nose Wart had found with his bare feet.

And that brings you up to speed, and back to the part where I am carrying dog poop in a plastic container, despite Lisa's insistence that I not.

***

"This is a bad idea, Ava," Lisa insisted as she caught up, still tugging on her coat against the evening chill of early November.

"Which is absolutely why I have to do it," I replied with a shrug.

"Morgan is on her way over to the house." Lisa grabbed my arm.

"That's what Aoife said," I agreed. And then I jumped up onto the roof.

I walked over to the chimney and pulled the Tupperware container out of one over-sized pocket. I don't actually need to wear a coat, unlike the Templar down in the yard currently pacing back and forth like an expectant father and rubbing her arms to try and ward off the cold that is sending her breath up in little puffs.

I stopped at the chimney and allowed myself to enjoy the smell of burning wood. Peering down the flue, I could see the embers below. That was good. I did not think this would work as well if they had a raging fire going.

I dumped the contents of the container down the throat of the chimney and then decided that the smeared Tupperware container would never be used again for holding anything that a human would want to consume, so I let that drop as well. On hindsight, I probably could have just thrown it in the trash when we got home.

"What the blazes was that!" Sugar Dumpling woofed around a mouthful of whatever she was currently consuming.

The sounds of the Danes barking like crazy came a split second later. Only, once again, I was able to understand what they were…saying.

"Squirrels? Is it squirrels?"

"Maybe it is a cat!"

"You chased all the cats away moons ago!"

"Yeah, well squirrels don't come out at night."

"Oh? And what makes you so smart?"

It continued on like that as I loped across the roof and leapt into the darkness. I landed beside Lisa who was already running like the wind for the house. She barely even twitched when I appeared at her elbow. Like she has ghouls appear out of the darkness all the time or something.

We both vaulted the barbed wire fence that separated our properties and altered our course just enough to align with the soft glow of our porch light.

In the distance behind us, I heard Sugar Dumpling bellowing, "I'ma callin' the po-leece!"

Sure enough, twenty minutes later, there were flashing red and blue lights in my long driveway. Not being an idiot (despite what some people might think) and actually being used to this sort of trailer trash mentality from my younger days, I'd already had Lisa touch up my paint. Also, I had these really funky John Lennon-style glasses that made me look more hip and less like a douche who wears her dark shades indoors.

Of course, when we opened the door, the responding officer had the role of douche all sewn up. He was a stereotype from his jack boots, to his huge gut that obscured any belt he might be wearing, to his mirrored shades that went out of style shortly after *Top Gun* hit the theaters, and finishing the look with his salt-and-pepper crew-cut. Keep in mind that we are in Oregon. Granted, we have moved out to the sticks just past good old Estacada, but we are still in the Pacific Northwest, not Backwater, Missouri.

"Seems we had a disturbance reported up this way, missy," Officer Nagel said. I know his name because it is on his name tag.

You know who else wears name tags at work? Fast food workers…grocery clerks…you know, the people who actually work their butts off for a living instead of sitting on it which is what I pictured Officer Nagel doing more often than not.

"Missy?" I had to fight the urge not to glare over my glasses at this guy. "Just hold—"

"You bought up the old Kirkpatrick place. Ain't seen no signs up yet about Christmas Trees." He ignored my comment and steamrolled right over me. "The Kirkpatricks always put on a helluva thing here. Hot chocolate for the kiddies, apple cider for the adults…a little snort of single malt for a select few."

The way he said it, I am sure he wanted me to believe he was one of those so-called select few. I had a hard time thinking he was as well liked as he seemed to believe he was.

"We won't be doing that." Lisa stepped up beside me.

Officer Nagel gave Lisa an up and down appraisal, then he returned his gaze to me, a nasty smirk on his face. "Your type always end up being tree huggers, don'tcha?"

"My *type*?" That second word dripped venom.

"You know…" His leer grew even wider as he waggled his eyebrows up and down. Then, as if to add emphasis, he brought his hands up as fists and bumped the insides together.

"Are you calling us les—" I started to rage, but before I could finish, a sweet melody drifted on the air. It pulled at my heart and made me swell with a joy that closed up my throat and made we want to weep and hug anybody close enough.

I was vaguely aware that a hand rested on my shoulder and gently guided me backwards until I was out of the doorway.

Something was making me feel very calm. I didn't like it one bit. I wanted to give that pig of a man a swift kick in the kenyakees (those would be his testicles in case you are confused).

"Is there a problem, Officer Nagel?" Aoife asked in a melodic voice that plucked the strings of my soul. It was as if I could not wait for the next words to fall from her mouth.

"Umm…err…no, ma'am," Officer Nagel stammered. He actually removed those ridiculous mirrored shades and tucked them into his pocket.

"Well then, perhaps you can go next door to the neighbors who called in the complaint and tell them that we would appreciate it if they would keep their dogs in their own yard." Aoife reached out and touched the man on his cheek causing him to blush like a schoolboy. I swear I saw a shimmer of purple emanate from Aoife's finger tips and dissolve into his skin.

"Yes, ma'am." The officer took a step back and his eyes narrowed as he looked in the direction of Richard and Sugar Dumpling's house. "They won't be bothering you anymore."

With that, Officer Nagel turned and practically staggered to his car. His steps were unsteady, and it almost looked as if he would topple over with the slightest touch.

Aoife turned to me and smiled, but that smile quickly turned to a look of concern…and almost fear. She grabbed me by the shoulders and gave me a gentle shake.

"Oh, miss, you shouldn't have been caught up in that." Aoife took my hand and led me to the living room where she sat me down on the couch.

Whoa! I heard Cody gasp. *That was intense.*

My head was clearing, but I could tell there was still a residue. Almost like a happiness hangover. I directed my intention inwards. I wish I could explain it, but it was like Cody was a little bundle of glee with a thick coating of infatuation.

"I don't understand," Aoife was apologizing. "That song should only work on males."

"And it did," I assured her. I reminded her of Cody's presence in my head.

"That is interesting," a voice said from the still open front door.

We all turned to discover Morgan standing there. This was her first official visit to the new house. Her eyes were scanning and her face was unemotional as always, but I still felt like there was a hint of disapproval as she took in the new digs.

"Come on in," I grumped. Although it was an unnecessary statement as she was already removing her coat and hanging it on the coat tree just inside the door.

"I see you have already made a nuisance of yourself," Morgan said as she closed the door.

"It wasn't my fault." Seriously, why would she automatically assume that I had done something wrong?

"Well, we don't have time to go into that right now." Morgan gave a dismissive wave of her hand and then looked like she was trying to find the least disgusting place that she could grace with her tiny butt.

It didn't matter that the furniture here was the exact same stuff that I'd had at the other house, I think she simply lumped everything in with the non-descript white farm house that was currently serving as my home. And I don't know who she thought she was in the first place; this house is only seventy or eighty years old. She had grown up in a freaking village over in Italy or some such place back when *THE* Jesus was healing lepers and all that stuff.

After finding a spot she apparently deemed the least offensive, she smoothed her dress under her and crossed her legs in that way all the classy ladies do in the movies. Hands folded neatly in her lap, she looked up at me.

"We have a Supernatural killer on the loose."

14

2

When the Children Cry

"Yeah?" I mean, seriously, what else was I gonna say?

"You don't watch the news at all, do you?" Morgan said this with her normal lack of emotion, but the disdain was clear.

"Too depressing." I gave a shrug.

Tell me if I am wrong here. Every time I turn on the local news, people are killing each other, abducting kids…or worse. And don't even get me started on the politicians. I refuse to even turn the idiot box on during election stuff. Did you see the story about the little girl who wrote her local politicians—I think they were senators or something—and said that they made her sad with all the negative talk? Democrat or Republican or Independent…they all say what they need to say in order to get you to like them, then nothing really changes no matter who you vote for.

All that said, I still vote. But it is mostly because of ballot measures and stuff. And since I actually read my pamphlet, I don't need a commercial to tell me what I think. Wow…how did I get here?

"Children are being killed."

See? THAT is why I don't watch the news. Who wants to sit down to dinner and hear that?

"When you say *children*…?"

"Seven so far." Morgan actually had a tinge of emotion in her voice. "All no older than eleven. The youngest was three."

"How do you know it is our fault?" I asked. "Last I checked, humans can be a pretty vile bunch."

"Hey!" Lisa objected.

"Westley Allen Dodd…Albert Fish…Ian Brady and Myra Hindley…" I started to tick off on my fingers.

"Okay!" Lisa snapped.

"Can we get back to the subject at hand?" Morgan asked, breaking the locked glare between me and Lisa.

"Please." I gave a rolling gesture with my hands.

"We know because we have an eyewitness." Morgan did not say a word, but my front door opened.

"Aren't you going to invite me in?" Belinda said with a lascivious wink.

"You have got to be kidding."

Standing in my doorway was the blond-haired, blue-eyed vampire that became my first Supernatural nemesis. She was dressed like a hooker pretending to be a schoolgirl. Her hair was a pair of braids on each side with the part down the middle in a razor-straight line that only the OCD of a vampire would have the patience to achieve. Seriously, if you were to take a measurement, I am willing to bet that it runs exactly down the center of the top of her head.

My eyes only paused for the briefest of seconds on the adorable saddle shoes she was wearing. Instead of the standard black and white, they were an emerald green and ruby red to match her plaid skirt and cotton blouse.

"Well?" Belinda said with a hint of agitation. And if she did not think I noticed her eyes dart over to Lisa, she would be very mistaken.

A little while ago, Lisa was supposedly meeting "in secret" with Belinda. I still have no idea what that might be about, and since I am trying to mend the rift that developed between Lisa and I, it has not been something that I have brought up. When she is ready, she will talk to me about it.

"Fine." I gave a wave with my hand.

"Belinda, please tell Ava what you saw," Morgan said after what seemed like an eternity of very uncomfortable silence.

"I believe we had an agreement."

Those words hung in the air with an almost physical presence. I thought I was the only one who gave Morgan a ration of grief. All the other Supernaturals that I had met up to this point had been very respectful and almost reverent when dealing with my regional Psychic (unless they were trying to kill her, but that was a rare occasion…so far).

"Now is not the time, Belinda," Morgan said, her lips pressed so tight that they practically disappeared from her face.

"Now is precisely the time," Belinda shot back. "You gave me your word."

I was a little surprised. I tried to imagine a situation where Morgan would either offer up freely or be coerced into "giving her word" to do anything. She was boss, and in my world, that meant she told people what to do and that was all there was to it.

"Lisa," Morgan said after what might have been just enough of a twitch around her eyes to count as a glare at Belinda, "Belinda requests for you to return to her residence to…work out the details of your agreement."

The old Ava would have blown a gasket. However, I was not going to say a word.

Oh, who am I kidding!

"What the hell agreement are you talking about?" I exploded. It was actually a second or two before I realized that my fingers and toes had gone switch. Yeah…I was pissed.

"This is between the human and me." Belinda gave a dismissive wave as she strutted past me and stopped in front of Lisa, her head tilting to one side like a puppy hearing a dog whistle.

I have no idea where it came from, but a growl escaped me that would have scared me if I had not been the one doing it. Faster than I think anybody gave me credit, I was between Belinda and Lisa, one switchfinger pressed into the soft spot under her chin.

"I don't know if it would kill you, but I am certain that it would at least sting a bit if I push all the way up into whatever passes for a brain in your pretty blond head," I snarled. Now, I know that word gets used a lot when people describe an angry person saying something, but I was seriously snarling.

"You think I'm pretty?" Belinda said with no more concern than if I might be simply offering her a cup of coffee.

"Children!" Morgan said with actual anger. This was out of character enough to make both Belinda and me turn to face her. "There is a monster in *my* district that is devouring children! Set your petty squabbles aside immediately and we can deal with all of this later."

When she put it like that, I was actually a little bit embarrassed. She had a point. After all, she had led off with the whole thing about something killing children, and here I was getting into it with the fanged she-bitch. Although, to be fair, she started it. At least that is how I remember it.

"And I am not a bargaining chip!" Lisa snapped.

The nasty look she shot Belinda made me smile. Take that, Fang Face!

"I said enough!" Morgan turned to Lisa, however, she was back to her level, unemotional self. Apparently Lisa did not merit the wrath of Morgan.

"So what did you see?" I willed my switch digits to retract, but I still could not help but smile when I saw just the smallest drop of blood well under Belinda's chin. To her credit, she did not even bother to wipe at it with her hand.

"I was up at Washington Park with my evening meal when I heard something from a nearby ravine. At first I ignored it, humans are always doing terrible things to each other, and I tend to make it none of my business. Only, despite what you might think, I will not ignore the cries of a child."

Belinda paused and stared at me like she was daring me to say anything to the contrary. Actually, I was too surprised at the admission to speak. After I kept my mouth shut, she resumed her narration.

"I bespelled my meal and went to investigate. Sadly, I was too late. I arrived just as the two tiny feet were vanishing down the gullet of the bitch."

If I did not know better, I would have thought that Belinda was actually just a bit upset. She sounded a little choked up, and her voice had changed to that strangled rasp people get when they are talking and trying not to cry.

"I was not sure what I was seeing at first. Honestly..." she took another deep breath and I actually caught my hand halfway to her shoulder where I would have tried to offer a conciliatory pat or something equally out of character, "...I honestly did not realize what I was seeing until that upper torso turned to me and fixed me with her eyeless gaze. Then I knew."

I heard Lisa gasp. I could see the grim expression that looked so out of place on Aoife's face. Heck, even Morgan seemed to be a little bit upset. That meant that yours truly was once again the idiot who had no idea what in the blazes Belinda was talking about.

"She is what is known as a lamia," Morgan said before I could ask my stupid question. "There are many myths about their origin, but the bottom line is this, they are the incarnation of evil. They are former women who were...indiscreet with married men who were fathers. According to the *Grimoire*, they made deals with a demon that would result in the man actually following through with what is usually the empty promise of leaving his spouse. They have their former upper body at its prime, but they are a serpent from the waist down."

"Yes, and this one took off down a drainage pipe the moment that she realized she had been spotted." Belinda actually shivered. "There was no way I was going to follow."

This was a lot to digest. I was not sure where to start. The whole snake-lady thing, the fact that Belinda had said she arrived just as the feet were vanishing down this thing's throat, or the fact that Belinda was too scared of it to pursue. We were not friends, but she did not strike me as a scaredy-cat.

"Wait!" I said as my mind snatched at something else Belinda had shared. "You said something about it being eyeless?"

"A lamia is tormented by nightmares whether she is awake

or asleep. Visions of the lives of the children that she destroyed and the children she would never be able to raise since her death in human form would come while in the act of labor during the birth of her first child," Lisa blurted.

All eyes turned her way. She blushed at the attention, but after rolling her shoulders back, she seemed to rise up just a bit taller before she spoke again.

"The deal with the demon ensures that she will marry the man and that she will become a mother. What they do not know is that they will never live to see a single day of that child's life. The nightmares and visions are said to drive them to the point where they gouge out their own eyes to try and avoid seeing the visions any longer. Unfortunately, that is when they discover that the visions will never subside as they play out in their minds forever. They eventually are driven to seek out and kidnap children, but they are so horrifying to look at that the children understandably scream and cry uncontrollably. They devour them, some say to keep their souls…much like a ghoul keeps other Supernaturals, in their mind."

I looked around and saw the same open-mouthed stares that I know I had on my face. That was a feat considering the company. Oh, getting my jaw to drop is really no big thing, but when you have Morgan and Belinda both slack-jawed with wonder, that is saying something.

"And where did you get your hands on a copy of the *Unnatural Grimoire?*" Morgan eventually rediscovered her ability to talk. Personally, that was not the question I had; in fact, it wasn't even in the top five.

"The only way Templars can effectively prepare for an enemy is to utilize every resource available." Lisa said it with a lot of hesitation in her voice. I had a funny feeling that she was not supposed to share her source. Only, when you thought about it, it made perfect sense.

"We can discuss that issue at a later time." Morgan was back to being as smooth as glass. "What else can you tell us?"

"Actually, there is not much more." Lisa shot me a look, but I had no guess as to what it meant.

"Wait!" Now I was ready to wade back in to this little conversation. "You said that the lamia thing was just finishing with swallowing a child." My attention was on Belinda now.

"Yes, the feet were just disappearing down her throat."

"So she what…opens her mouth like a snake or something?"

"As far as I could tell."

"And you are here sending me after this thing why exactly?" It was now time to poke Morgan for a few minutes.

"That is the role of a ghoul. You are, for lack of a better term, the hired muscle. Ghouls are responsible for eliminating rogues and anything that may bring harm to a region of the employing Psychic."

I noticed her wording. She used the term "employing" because she had not claimed me specifically for her district. Of course, I was bothered at first, but I have learned why and am okay with it now.

"So you want me to…" I guess I still needed to hear Morgan say it in order to make it real.

"Hunt down and kill this creature."

"No talking or maybe trying to capture her and possibly have Betty create a cell. Just—"

"There is no need. A lamia will not be reasoned with or convinced to do anything. They are mad with grief and anger." Morgan amazed me at how she could say these sorts of things with next to no emotion in her voice.

I guess that was it. Now for the ugly part of the business. Well, not actually ugly, but maybe uncomfortable would be a better term.

"And what does this job pay upon completion?" I had learned that it is best to get specific terms with Morgan. She is good at changing the game just when you think that you have crossed the finish line. "And by completion, I mean, when I kill *this* lamia, I bring you the head or whatever and you make the arrangements however you do them and this job is done."

It might seem like I was being silly, but I'd been working with Morgan for a little while now and knew that she had a way of telling me that a job was still not finished when I would report in and tell her that it was.

"The head will suffice," Morgan agreed with a slight nod. "And the pay will be a base of one million dollars, but that amount will be decreased by a hundred thousand with each subsequent child death that is reported and can be attributed to this lamia."

That seemed kind of vague. I mean, how would she know if some child's death could be pinned on this lamia. Obviously, that was written on my face.

"I am receiving…ripples would perhaps be the best way to describe it to you, each time a child dies. My only guess is that it is something emanating from the creature."

Fair enough. Sure, some random tragedy could strike and she could deduct money, but that was definitely not Morgan's style. I could at least trust her in this regard. She was always pretty generous with the payments. It was really just a matter of her accepting my version of done.

With the details ironed out, I figured we were finished. I stood for a moment waiting for Morgan and Belinda to leave. For several seconds, nobody moved.

"We can speak outside," Lisa finally said, leading Belinda to the front door.

I wanted to protest, but I did not really have any grounds. Lisa could do as she pleased. Our issue had come down to my trusting her. Admittedly, that was difficult for me in any regard and with any individual before she became a Templar. Now that she was a member-in-training for the organization that had tried to eradicate all of ghoul-kind that now apparently had a price on my head specifically, it was understandably strained.

Morgan stood motionless like a porcelain statue until the door shut; then she fixed me with her gaze. "Lisa is obviously proceeding with her training."

It wasn't a question, but there was just the slightest lilt to her voice that might be her either asking me or showing some level of concern. Since I had no idea what she wanted, I stood quietly and waited for her to continue or simply leave in the blink of an eye like she so often did.

"And has Race been trying to put an end to this ridiculous bounty on your head?"

"As far as I know." He was practically as bad as Morgan when it came to *not* telling me things. However, I was almost touched that Morgan said it was a ridiculous bounty.

"And we still have the Claude situation to deal with, but that all needs to be shelved. This takes priority," Morgan said. When she took my hands in hers, I almost shed my skin. "I need you to make this happen quickly, Ava."

Besides the fact that children were being killed, I'd heard enough to know that a lamia was nasty. Seriously, the whole having an affair with a married man was bad in and of itself. Breaking up a family was wicked. But making a deal with a demon to ensure that the man actually left his family was abhorrent. And then to stack on having her own baby with the guy as part of the deal? Seriously, who does that?

Oh…wait. Lamia's do it.

"I will handle it." I wanted to have something snappy or witty to come back with, but I couldn't think of anything.

I blinked. I swear that was all I did. And in that amount of time, Morgan was gone. I really wish that I knew how she did that.

If you ate her, I bet you would find out.

How long have you been out, Blodwen? I asked.

Long enough to hear that a lamia is loose. Nasty creatures those.

Then you also know I have been tasked to kill her.

I was growing to sort of like the old gwyll. Blodwen was settling in nicely as a permanent resident of my head. The fact that a ghoul absorbed the essence of certain Supernaturals and that their souls, or whatever you want to call them, took up residence in my head was something that I was starting to get accustomed to. Also, I was really getting the hang of being able to communicate with them without talking out loud…or looking like I was either constipated or trying to figure out a really hard calculus problem without a calculator.

The door opened and Lisa stepped back inside, patting her

arms and I saw little flakes of white brush away. That could only mean—

"It's snowing." Lisa's nose was a bright red and her cheeks were all rosy from the cold. Her smile was so warm that I did not think it was possible for a chill to reach her.

"Does it look like it is sticking?"

I felt just a little nibble of happiness fill in the cracks that had been etched on my soul these past weeks and months. I always loved snow. There was just something so peaceful and settling about it. Add in the beauty of a world blanketed in pure white, and what was there not to like? Well, except for having to drive in it. The Portland-Metro area in Oregon is not really known for snow. Drivers here all turned into absolute idiots whenever there is a drastic change in weather. There would be no way in hell I would take my precious Corvette out in this sort of thing.

"Yep. We should see a few inches by the look of things."

Lisa walked past me and I could tell she had something on her mind. Still, she did not say a word as she went into the kitchen where Aoife had retreated and was currently making some sort of stew on the stove.

I debated for a few seconds and then finally followed her in. Screwing my mouth down so that, hopefully, I did not go too far, I slipped into a seat at the kitchen's little breakfast nook and folded my hands in front of me.

"You ready to tell me what else you know about lamias?" I asked.

It was like I had flicked a switch. Aoife turned off the burner, removed her big pot and left the room. Lisa stood with her back to me, her face reflected perfectly in the window that looked out across a rolling hill of growing pine trees that would never see the inside of a house except maybe for firewood. I was not exactly sure what the faeries' mindset was when it came to fires. And it wasn't like I needed a fire to get warm, but they did look and smell nice.

"This thing has no known weakness. They die of grief."

I heard what Lisa said, but I was not really registering it.

There was something about her answer that gave me a chill. I was about to press the issue when she continued.

"The Templars have other resources besides the *Grimoire*. And one of the first things you learn is the weakness and how to kill whatever creature it is that you are looking up."

It dropped like a lead balloon. She was telling me without actually telling me that the Templars knew how to kill practically everything they came up against. Considering the fact that ghouls were their number one target, that would lead me to believe—

"Ghouls, vampires," Lisa turned to face me, "even psychics are listed. There is an appendix with a list of monsters that have no known weaknesses or sure methods of elimination. Lamias are on that list."

I absolutely noticed the very slight pause before she said the word "elimination." She was trying her best to be politically correct, or whatever this could be called. The problem with that was the fact that I do not follow those same conventions.

"So do you have all the ghoul killing methods committed to memory?" Stupid Ava! Why can't I ever learn to keep my big mouth shut? To her credit, I barely noticed the flinch that passed over Lisa's face.

"Can we worry about that later? Right now you need to know that you are going after something that nobody has been able to kill. We are talking about a creature that has records of existence going back centuries." Lisa's voice became strangled and I thought that she might break into tears. "And they are not a defenseless creature."

"Obviously," I snorted, trying to laugh off her serious tone and dire sounding warning, "they eat children. You really have to be something special to hurt or kill children."

"They don't seem to feel any forms of physical pain," Lisa insisted, undeterred by my dismissive attitude. "There are reports of them being the second most resilient creature when it comes to damage."

"Second to what?"

"Ghouls."

"See!" I pointed with one hand and touched a finger from the other to the tip of my nose. "That must mean that we are tougher."

I will admit that my logic was faulty at best, but the last thing that I needed in my head when going into a fight was a big, Thanksgiving Day-sized scoop of doubt. I had plenty of that on my own without others feeding the monster.

"Just be careful."

"Hey," I tried to give a lopsided grin that would make Han Solo proud, "it's me!"

Lisa left the kitchen. I could tell that she was unimpressed. And now that I was alone, I had to admit, she had done her job if her job had been to make me nervous. My mind drifted over to another track as well.

Morgan was never one who was not in the know. She seemed surprised by Lisa's little dictionary recital on the lamia. Since I had no idea what the Grimoire said, I had to think that perhaps the Templars might have more of an inside track in the knowledge department on this particular beastie.

There was only one thing I could do. Pulling out my phone, I scrolled through my contacts. There it was: Race Mitchell.

3

Runaway

I tapped the screen and put the phone to my ear. It picked up on the third ring. Race sounded out of breath. My mind immediately pictured him dripping wet, draping the towel that he had just wiped the sweat from his face over one shoulder. Oh, and he was not wearing a shirt.

"Ava Birch, to what do I owe the pleasure?" Race asked.

"So my calls are a pleasure?" I actually slapped my forehead with the palm of my hand. That second or two of silence seemed to last an eternity.

"At least this way I know you are still alive and well," Race said with nothing in his voice to lead me to believe that he felt anything other than some sense of duty or responsibility in this task of his to try and get my name off the Templar's Most Wanted.

"You do remember that I am a ghoul." If he wasn't going to show any interest, then I was not going to act like an idiot. "I stopped being alive a long time ago. The sooner you lock onto that little fact, the better."

Umm, okay, that did not mean I needed to be a bitch. I was seriously no good at banter or small talk. Best to simply get to the point.

"I actually called with a purpose. You are no doubt aware of the series of child murders happening in the area?"

"Does the news talk about anything else?" he asked with a sarcastic bite to his voice.

Actually, I didn't know. Seeing as how I don't watch the news, I had to imagine that his point was valid. I mean, since the reason that I didn't watch local (or cable) news was because they were to journalism what Snookie and J-Wow are to music television, I simply did not see the point.

"Well we have reason to believe that we know the culprit." I could almost feel Race leaning into the phone as he waited for me to reveal the answer. "Lamia."

There was a long enough pause that I thought he might have hung up. Then he spoke. "Are you absolutely certain?"

"We have an eyewitness of sorts. So yes, we are as certain as we can be, I imagine."

"And let me guess." There was a snort that could have been a laugh from his end. "Morgan has sent you after the creature."

It wasn't like it was any big secret. He knew full well that I worked for the Psychic. He also was probably more aware than I was as to the role of a ghoul in the employ of a regional Psychic.

"The contract has been offered, yes."

"Don't do it, Ava."

For the first time ever, I thought that I detected just a hint of concern in Race's voice. He might have even sounded scared. I quickly dismissed that notion. Mostly because I did not want to know what in this world could scare a man like Race Mitchell. For a man who had stepped up to go toe-to-toe with an adult fiery jötunn, he suddenly sounded like he was more than just a little bit worried.

"I think you underestimate my abilities." There, that sounded confident without being too cocky; or at least that was what I was going for.

"No, actually, I think you are underestimated by just about everybody *except* me."

Hmm. Well that caught me by surprise. Race Mitchell thought that I was capable? What more could a woman ask for in a man. Well, except for rugged good looks, a body chiseled from granite and hands that looked strong enough to crack walnuts while being gentle enough—

"Ava?" Aoife was at my shoulder.

I instantly felt like I had just been caught with my hands down my pants. What? Guys think they are the only ones who ever get caught tending to their own gardens? The only reason you get caught more often is because you can't keep your hands off the little soldier. Women are more discreet and can show at least a certain degree of restraint. But rest assured, you don't think that all those neck massagers are really being used to massage necks, do you? And don't get me started on shower head attachments.

"What is it, Aoife?" I tried not to show embarrassment or annoyance. While I was pretty sure that I didn't blush, I knew that I was terrible at hiding my emotions either on my face or in my voice.

"Lisa is gone."

"What do you mean?"

"I mean that the girl has left. When I asked where she was going, she told me to butt out." Aoife blushed with what looked like embarrassment. "I had simply told her that she should not do anything rash or hasty, that you would be fine."

"Which way did she go?" She did not have a car, so it was not like she could have gone far.

Aoife was now obviously uncomfortable. I had a feeling there was something that she was not telling me.

"Ava?" Race was almost shouting and I quickly brought the phone back up to my ear.

I guess that is mostly habit. I mean, I can hear a conversation between two people at the other side of the food court at the mall if I concentrate.

"What?" I held a finger up to Aoife so that she would hold on just a second before answering.

"What did that girl mean, Lisa is gone?"

Okay, here is the deal. If he was listening, then he knows just as much as I do at this particular moment. Why do people do that? Why do they ask a person standing right beside them who has seen the exact same thing a stupid question like "What's happening?" I can't be the only one who thinks that is absolutely idiotic.

"She was just getting to that, so if you would be quiet?" I returned my attention to Aoife.

"She called somebody and…" Aoife's voice trailed off and I was becoming more than just a little concerned.

"Start talking, siren," I growled.

"She called somebody and a pair of gargoyles showed up not more than few minutes later. I tried to talk her out of it."

"Did she—" Race's voice was almost shouting in my ear, but I was one step ahead of him.

"Gargoyles? Did you say gargoyles?"

Really? Not for nothing, but I have lived most of my life in ignorant bliss. Now, monsters just seem to be coming out of the woodwork. Gargoyles, lamias, vampires. What's next?

"They came down, picked her up, and flew off." Aoife was wringing her hands. "I tried to talk her out of it, but she said that she was not just going to sit back and let you get killed."

"So, what? She is gonna get herself killed instead?" I snapped.

Not thinking about it, I tapped the button on my phone and hung up on Race. When I walked into the living room, I almost tripped over a trio of goblins busily scrubbing up the poop tracks that Nose Wart had left on the floor. It only took a second for me to realize something else.

"Where is Nose Wart?"

Here is the deal, ever since the goblins moved in, Nose Wart has been some sort of leader. I never thought to ask, but it seems that he has taken that role upon himself and acts as the liaison between me and the pack. He even speaks on behalf of the bugbears.

As a group, every single goblin took off for the basement. They were all gibbering wildly in nothing resembling a language that I could decipher. When I reached the door, a bugbear was hurrying up the stairs. As soon as he saw me—I am assuming it is a he because I have yet to discover what might make the difference between a male and female bugbear—the creature dropped to the floor and extended its arms like it was praying or something. A plaintive howl made me stop in my tracks.

"Quickly, miss!" Aoife was whispering in my ear. "They believe that they have incurred your wrath and are begging for their lives."

"Seriously?" I spun on the siren. "What the hell did I do now?" All I wanted to know is where Nose Wart had vanished to as well as Lisa? I pursed my lips as a notion took hold. "Did they leave together?"

Aoife nodded. From down in the basement, I could hear what sounded like somebody throwing an entire kitchen's worth of pots and pans against the wall.

"Oh dear," Aoife whispered.

"Now what?" Did everybody lose their minds all of a sudden? I did not have time for this sort of thing.

"They are preparing for battle, miss." I turned to Aoife with a look that I hope expressed the fact that she needed to be a little more specific. "They believe that you are about to execute them all. No goblin will simply accept death without a fight no matter the circumstance. If you are about to kill them all, then they are preparing to fight to the death."

"Shall I go down and rip them to shreds?" the bugbear asked, sounding almost hopeful.

"Everybody just wait!" I shouted. My voice seemed to reverberate through the entire house. "First off, nobody is being torn to shreds. I am not preparing to execute any of you. All I want are answers. Where is Lisa? Where is Nose Wart? Is that so difficult?"

"Yes," Aoife answered very matter-of-factly. "It is extremely difficult when nobody has an answer."

I planted my hands on my hips. After a few deep, cleansing breaths, I cleared my throat and spoke in as neutral of a tone as I could manage.

"Then perhaps somebody could simply say so and we would not be wasting all of this time. Lisa could be anywhere by now."

I felt my anger start to try and flare up, and I immediately shut my mouth.

"You must excuse them, miss." Aoife placed a hand on my shoulder and leaned so close to my ear that I swear I could feel her lips. "Ghouls are known to use extreme measures in order to discover what they need to know."

I sighed. Lisa was already gone. I would go find her, but I needed to put an end to this ridiculous nonsense. I could not have goblins preparing to fight to the death every time I lost my temper. Those poor things would be spending all their time suiting up for battle.

"Everybody into the living room, right now!"

Without another word, I spun on my heel and stalked into the front room. Any other time and it would have been cute, or even humorous. Over three dozen goblins, a handful of bug-bears, a trio of adolescent fiery jötunn, and a siren all crowded in. Actually, the jötunn sort of hunkered down at each exit. In my head, I felt Cody and Blodwen perk up. Yep, that was pretty much everybody that mattered.

"First things first," I let my gaze drift around the room, "just because I get angry, that does not mean anybody is about to be killed. At least nobody in this house."

"But is it not the way of the ghoul to destroy all who stand against or fail them?" a bugbear growled.

"Probably," I said with a shrug. "But you are all under my roof. That makes you part of this growing family of dysfunction. Are there any questions?"

When nobody spoke up, I continued; returning now to the important matter of Lisa…and Nose Wart as well.

"Can anybody tell me where Lisa and Nose Wart have run off to?" I asked.

"With the gargoyles," a goblin squeaked.

"Right, and does anybody know where the gargoyles took them?"

"Up," another goblin offered.

After a deep breath, I reworded my question. "And what destination might they be headed for?"

"North," a jötunn spoke up.

That was at least something, but now I had enough information to call this little meeting to an end. I was about to dismiss them when one of the goblins stood and walked right up to me. It was one of the females.

"I am Butt Pimple, dame to Nose Wart, leader of the Goblin Vomit clan…"

Wait, when did they change their name? When I met Nose Wart, he had said he was from the Cow Fart clan. I would ask later.

"Yes?" I knelt down to be eye level with this goblin. "Something that you want to say?"

"Our clan leader and I have rutted and put me with a litter."

She said that like it meant more than just what I was hearing. Obviously there was more to this story. Then Aoife appeared beside me again. She took the female goblin's hands and then turned to me with a huge smile.

"We are very fortunate," the siren exclaimed. When I gave her a nod to please explain, she did so. "She will know where her mate is. Or, at least she will know the general direction. They are bonded as long as she is carrying children. If he dies, she will feel that bond sever. That will allow her to seek proper vengeance. Some say that it was a wish from a dying goblin queen granted by a demon who was indebted to the—"

"Okay, got it." I hated cutting Aoife off like that, but I can only handle so much of this Supernatural history at any given time. Besides, it is likely that I will forget it anyway. " Short version…goblins have some sort of internal compass that points to the direction of their mate. Understood."

"Well it's not quite as simplistic or crude as that," Aoife sniffed, her hurt feelings obvious by the whispery tone of her voice that sounded on the verge of tears. "But if that helps you understand, then it will suffice."

"So…did you say your name was…" I left it open as a lead, but goblins are not good at such subtle things. "Butt Pimple?"

"Yes, Just Ava."

Do their parents just use some sort of Mad Libs naming process where they choose an ugly body part and couple it with some form of skin condition? I added that to my list of things I needed to ask when life settled down to some sort of normal.

"If I bring you with me, can you lead me to Nose Wart?" I asked.

"Yes, Just Ava," the female goblin snorted. Oh yeah, goblins snort. Of course they make a wide variety of odd noises along with some very unpleasant smells, but that is beside the point.

"Then let's go."

I headed for my garage and stopped when I realized that I was the only one moving. Everybody else was basically frozen in place.

"They told me that you had moved out here," a vaguely familiar voice said. "And I see that you have begun to build your army."

I felt Blodwen perk up in my head. *Magic...very strong magic*, she warned.

I turned to the source of the voice and saw a large orange tabby perched on the back of my sofa. It was licking its paws in that way cats do when they are grooming themselves and trying to pretend that they are the only one in the room.

In a shimmer of what I guess had to be magic, the cat morphed into a woman with hair the color of real rubies. Oh, and it was shiny enough that prisms of light reflected from it in a rainbow of light that acted almost as an aura around her. The woman was slight and had that wicked sexuality flashing in her eyes.

"Rosanna?" I cocked my head to one side.

I'd met her the night of my showdown in the graveyard with Adrianna, The Queen of the Zombies, and current inmate in a cell in my head. She'd actually been the one to report zombies in Estacada after one of the early failed constructs trampled through her garden or some such thing.

"I heard that somebody bought this place." The woman hopped off the counter.

"Did you freeze everybody in my house?"

34

"Oh!" She looked just a bit embarrassed. "Sorry about that. I detected a lot of Supers and was not about to pop in and be some vampire kiss' dinner. I had no idea that it was you and…" She slipped past me and squealed. "Jötunn? You have three fiery jötunn? And are those bugbears!"

She was like a child in a toy store as she darted around the room. She was about to pick up Butt Pimple when a hand shot out and grabbed her by the throat.

"Aoife!" I barked, surprised by her hostile reaction. In fact, that was the first time that I'd seen her use any sort of physical attack.

"She's a *witch*, miss."

Aoife began to glow an ugly shade of purple. That is saying something since I love purple and did not ever think I could see an ugly hue in that color. Oh, and by glow, I don't mean that her skin was turning color like when a person gets angry or embarrassed. What I mean is that she was becoming a walking glow stick.

"I realize that, Aoife." When did I become a peace maker? I am usually the one flying off the handle. "She is not an enemy."

"Witches are always the enemy of a siren."

No addressing me as "miss" or anything of the sort. Nope, she was one pissed off girl. I actually felt a chill roll off of Aoife, and I could swear that I smelled the ocean.

"Okay, short version." I needed to find a class or something. There was just too much in the Supernatural world for me to ever feel like I would catch up with the learning curve.

"They made us."

At least I have learned enough about the Supernatural world to realize that she was being quite literal. The only thing was that now was simply not the time. With each passing second, Lisa was getting farther away. If she was doing something stupid like going after this lamia on her own, then she might die—yes, Nose Wart was supposedly with her, but goblins are really little more than cannon fodder.

"We can worry about that later," I snapped. When she still did not let go, I decided to play my ghoul card. "If Lisa dies because we wasted time with this nonsense, I will rip your heart out of your chest."

Wow. I have no idea where that came from. Seriously, I was just going to try to talk tough and be a bit of a bully. In any case, it worked. Aoife released Rosanna and turned to me, little drops of silver leaking from the corners of her eyes.

"Apologies, miss."

"We will deal with this later," I assured. "But at the moment, my top concern is Lisa and making sure that fool girl has not gone off and gotten herself killed…or worse."

Was there something worse than killed? Considering all I have seen in such a short span, I tend to think so. I pushed that thought out of my head. Now was not the time.

"Am I missing something?" Rosanna asked.

Again, I did not have time for a long retelling of the events as they have happened thus far to get her up to speed.

"Gargoyles took Lisa," I said as I headed to the garage.

One of the things that is a must when you live out in the sticks is a pickup truck or other such vehicle. As soon as I settled on this house, I had picked up an old Ford Ranger. Tan, non-descript, and about fifteen years old with a small camper shell over the bed; it was exactly what I needed.

As I climbed in the driver's seat, I was a little surprised when Aoife actually popped the passenger seat so that Rosanna could climb in when it appeared that she was coming with us. Also, Butt Pimple scurried in so that she could be in the cab as well. I needed to get my head straight. I'd damn near rushed out and left the only source I had that could lead me to where Nose Wart—and hopefully Lisa—were located.

"Buckle up for safety," I sing-songed as I started her up and hit the button on my garage door opener.

I heard a clatter behind me and looked over my shoulder to see a dozen goblins piling in the bed of the truck. I guess Rosanna had dropped whatever spell she had used to freeze everybody. It also looked like I would be rolling in with plenty of back-up.

As I turned onto the road, I took a few seconds to give Rosanna a little more info. Her being a witch and all, maybe she could offer help. I was just getting to the good part as we reached the intersection that would lead down the mountain and to the freeway.

"…so the word is there is a lamia, and that is where we believe all these missing children might be connected," I was saying.

"Stop the car!" Rosanna yelped. Seriously, she sounded like somebody had just punched her in the gut.

More out of reflex, my foot hit the brakes. The truck fishtailed slightly in the half inch of snow that was already frosting this untraveled road. I looked over my shoulder.

"Let me out…NOW!" Rosanna was punching the back of the front seat where Aoife was sitting.

Aoife glanced at me and I nodded. She opened the door, a blast of cold came sweeping in, eating all the warm air from the heater. She hopped out and flipped the lever that made the passenger seat fall forward. Rosanna exited like she was shot from a cannon.

"I hope that you know what you are doing," Rosanna huffed, vapor rolling from her mouth and nose in little puffs that were snatched away by the wind that was making the snow look like it was falling horizontally.

"I know exactly what I am doing," I replied as Aoife got back into the truck. "I am going after my friend Lisa Jenkins."

"If you are going after her, that is fine, but if you think she went after this lamia, then I leave you with this warning, do not look into the eye sockets of the lamia. If you do, she will be able to overwhelm you with her despair and sap your will to fight." Rosanna reached into her shirt and produced a necklace with a large yellow sun that looked like it had been made by a grade school student on 'macaroni art' day. "And I also give you this." She removed the ridiculous necklace and handed it to Aoife to give to me.

"Umm…thanks?" I held it up and examined it in the light of the truck's cab.

"It is a luck charm," Rosanna said with obvious pride in her voice.

"I know I am only going to sound like an idiot."

Rosanna held up a hand to stop me. "All you need to do is put the sun in your mouth and bite down. That will invoke it. Use it if you are in a difficult situation and it might help sway events by some random thing that alters your potentially bad outcome and turns it…more positive."

As vague as that sounded, beggars can't be choosers. "Thanks." I put it over my head and let it fall into place after I swept my hair up. Tucking the sun into my blouse, I gave a wave.

Aoife pulled the door shut and I slipped the truck back into drive. As we turned left and started for the freeway, I looked in my rearview mirror. Rosanna was still standing in the middle of the road. It was as if the darkness swallowed her up when she disappeared from view. She did not so much fade as she just was not there anymore.

I would have to ask her later about that freeze thing she did before entering my house. If that was another charm, I would absolutely be buying a few.

"Will you be having *her* over often?" Aoife whispered. There was venom in her tone that just did not fit the creature that I had come to know.

"We will talk about that later," I said. "Butt Pimple, where are we headed?"

A stubby and gnarled claw of a hand pointed off to the right. I was just reaching the bottom of the hill where the highway that led either up to the mountains or down to the Portland-Metro area crossed my path. I turned right towards Portland.

4

The Zoo

The roads were mostly empty. Oregonians are not great drivers when the white stuff falls. I certainly would not be out if it weren't an emergency. As I cruised along, the road in front of me almost reduced to a tunnel as the headlights hit the falling snow and reflected the light back at me. I could actually see better with the headlights off, but I am sure that other cars on the road might not appreciate it.

As I reached the interstate, I was now faced with a new dilemma. Thankfully, a hand shot over my shoulder and indicated that I once again go right which would have me headed northbound in I-205.

"So what is the deal with sirens and witches?" I asked.

Heck, we had a few minutes, and I could tell that Aoife was still steaming; she had not complained at all about my driving. And considering I was driving a Ford Ranger like it was my shiny Corvette…in the snow…it was pretty obvious something was gnawing at her.

"Hecate," Aoife said. Yep, she said it like I had some idea of who she was talking about.

"The first witch," Butt Pimple breathed.

Great, I thought, *the goblin knew what Aoife is talking about*. I decided to hurry this along.

"Just pretend that I am ignorant to everything that you are talking about and give me the story," I said with as much dignity that one as ill-informed as I could manage.

"She was granted an island by a king after she removed the hex that was causing all his wives to suffer stillborns."

I made no comment about the part in regards to the *all* the king's wives line. See how good I am getting at this listening and not interrupting thing?

"As she would travel about and offer her services in magic, Hecate began to gain not only fame, but also considerable treasure. She would return to her island every so often to drop it off before going away once more. At first, she was content with a few hired men. And since she took the only ship on the island each time she left, effectively stranding her guards until she returned, she believed that her treasure was safe.

"One time, she returned from abroad with chests of gold and a variety of exotic things to discover her island empty. In a fit of anger, Hecate took four slave girls and performed a series of rituals on them—"

"Creating sirens!" I blurted.

"Yes," Aoife said with obvious sadness. "And in her creation, she instilled the ability for us to sing. But her lack of trust prompted her to twist in a single curse as well. Every year, we are compelled to return to the island of our origin where we give birth. If it is a girl, she is raised and taught the ways of The Songs. A coven of witches live on that island to this day to teach new sirens how to use their voice."

I was not so dense that I did not hear the underlying tone in her voice that spoke of something horrible. This would be where she dropped the bomb. Still, I had to ask after a few seconds passed where I was becoming certain that she did not want to tell the rest.

"And do sirens ever give birth to a boy?"

Aoife sniffed hard and the drops of silver were flowing freely from her eyes. I was trying to keep my eyes on the road, but I was able to take one hand off the steering wheel long enough to give what I hoped was a pat of consolation.

"They do…and that is the horror of the curse."

I wanted to ask. I mean, wouldn't you at this point? Still, I kept quiet and waited for her to reveal what I now knew was going to be a horrible admission.

"Hecate never forgave the men who stole from her. So, when she made us her island guardians, we were cursed to be compelled to kill any male child that we conceived. When the babe is birthed and the gender revealed, they are either swept up and taken to be trained as sirens, or we must take the male babe to the water and submerge them, burn the corpse, and then scatter the ashes over a garden that she has kept all these years."

That final part sunk in a bit slow. At last, I asked, "You mean she is alive to this day? This Hecate woman still exists?"

"Some say that she absorbs the souls of the male children, while others believe that it is through her garden that she continues on. In any case, she is the fountainhead of magic for the modern day earth witches," Aoife sniffed.

"But why hate Rosanna for something that this Hecate woman does?"

"Because, they all must attend her at some point when they complete their induction ceremonies and are accepted by witchkind as one of their own. During that trip, they all attend one of the ash sprinkling rituals."

Jeez, I thought, *this Supernatural community is more messed up than humans sometimes…and that takes serious effort.*

"And do they know where these ashes come from that are sprinkled on the garden?" I asked.

Aoife opened her mouth to reply, but then snapped it shut. I shot her a glance and noticed that she was in deep thought. Just then, a little goblin claw shot past my face and pointed to an exit. Thank goodness nobody else was on the road, or at least in my vicinity. I jerked, and the wheel turned sharp for a split second, causing the truck to slide. By the time I was back in control of the vehicle, I was one lane over and still kind of wobbly. I swear, if my heart still beat, it would be in my throat right this minute.

I slowed and took the exit that Butt Pimple had indicated. I was down to about ten miles per hour by the time I reached the overpass. I knew all too well about how overpasses are usually much worse than roads in foul weather. This one proved no exception. It might have actually been one solid sheet of ice. I did not get out of the truck to check, but I did slide sideways for about half the length until I sort of ricocheted off one curb. Just as I was about to lose all forward momentum, I was across and back on just plain old snow.

"I can be so stupid," I muttered.

"What do you mean?" Aoife asked.

"Belinda said that she was at Washington Park when she spotted the lamia."

Aoife looked at me with a blank expression that made it clear that she was not sure what my point might be. I indicated towards the sign that said we were approaching Washington Park as well as the Portland Zoo.

"They are near," Butt Pimple whispered.

I started up the winding road that took us to the massive parking lot near the zoo's entrance. The lighting was amplified to a brilliant glare as the yellowish streetlights reflected off the inch or two of snow that had already fallen in just a short time.

"You stay in the truck," I said to Aoife. "If I am not back in an hour, call Race and tell him where I was last seen. Tell him that I went in search of Lisa."

"You want me to call that Templar?" Aoife gasped. Obviously she did not agree with my instructions.

I had a really bad feeling. I was not sure if it was some sort of ghoul sense trying to warn me, but it was twisting in my belly. I wanted to make sure that somebody capable was alerted if this went bad. Not wanting to waste any more time than I already had with everything else up to this point, I just gave Aoife a sharp nod and got out of the truck with Butt Pimple right on my heels.

She sniffed the air and then started to zig and zag as we headed up towards the zoo entrance. It would figure, as we reached the locked gate, there was a sudden series of shrieks, roars, and growls like every single animal was jolted awake at once. I don't know any other way to describe it, but I could tell by the sounds drifting on the night that there was something *very* bad nearby.

I stopped at the gate and had to push myself to vault up and over. Something was filling me with a terrible dread. It was overwhelming and so incredibly foreign that I think the only reason that I was able to keep going was out of sheer ignorance. I honestly had never felt so much fear since becoming a ghoul.

The best I can compare it to from my human days would be that time I was working as a bartender in this little place in downtown Portland. The only place employees could park was this lot about a block from one of the homeless shelters. Nothing against the homeless, they have enough problems of their own, but when you are a twenty-something-year-old girl all alone at three in the morning and a pair of rough looking fellas are staggering behind you as you cross the dark, empty lot where your car is the only one and you don't have mace, a Taser, or even some pepper spray, your heart rate kicks into a new gear.

Where is all of this negativity coming from? I asked inwardly.

It is the dread, Blodwen said with a tremor rippling in her own voice.

The dread? I asked as I scooped up Butt Pimple and started off into the eerie darkness of the zoo.

The lamia is a sad creature. She has been forced to see all the pain she caused as well as the torment of visions of a life she can never have. Blodwen's voice was now becoming distant, like she was at the end of a long hallway. *I have sent Cody to his room and I will be securing myself as well.*

Wait…what? I came to a sudden halt.

The dread of a lamia seeps through all realms of the Supernatural. You will have enough trouble overcoming it on your own. If Cody and I are swept away by it, it may be too much for you to handle.

And then she was gone. I had not known that the residents of my head could seal themselves away from me. Learn something new every day, I guess.

"Down there," Butt Pimple hissed in my ear. I'd placed her on my shoulders much like a human parent might do their child while strolling through the Portland Zoo. "It is just down at the bottom of that trail."

Of course, I could see perfectly. My ghoul vision allowed me to see in the dark just as if it were normal daylight. That didn't make the path any less scary. Something was down there.

I was moving really slow. Seriously, rushing into something like this would probably not go well. Also, Butt Pimple was starting to shiver.

"Are you cold?" I whispered.

"N-n-no, Just Ava."

The goblin shifted on my shoulders and her clawed hands started to dig in around my neck. If I needed to breathe, I would have been in big trouble. As it was, I simply brought my hands up and tried to gently pry hers loose.

When that scream cut through the night, it was like a razor being taken to a balloon. My reaction was sudden and all thoughts of caution vanished. I took off at a sprint, my switch fingers and toes coming out in a flash. My feet were literally making sparks as I dug into the paved path.

I came to a T-intersection and sniffed. Something foul was nearby. My head snapped to the right and I took off towards the sounds of renewed screaming.

I was in no way prepared for what I discovered in a small clearing. Having never seen a lamia before, I guess I really did not know what to expect.

She was all woman from about the waist on up. I'll get back to that part in a second. It was the lower half that had my attention. Coiled two or three times at the base was what could only be called a snake body. It was a sickly gray streaked with black and I could see dark purple veins pulsing just under the scaly surface. If the snake part were stretched out, I would imagine the length to be about thirty feet or so.

And then there was the upper torso. She was a brunette with shoulder length hair. Naked, her breasts had yet to be subjected to enough gravity for them to sag. They were almost perfect. I say almost because of the dark green fluid leaking from them that was a bit off-putting. Sure, shape-wise they were perfect grapefruit halves with irritatingly perfect nipples. Only, I could not get past that green stuff. Yuck!

I saved her face for last because it really took me a few seconds to realize all that was wrong with that picture. The easy part was the eyes. Actually, it was the lack of eyes. They had been savagely gouged out, and the hollows were ugly, raw craters that wept pus and blood, leaving tear streaked stains down her cheeks. Her lips were full and I would have guessed them to be surgically enhanced or whatever it was that women did to try and get them that full. Only, these looked…natural. Take the eyes out of the picture and I bet she had been a stunner when she was human.

Oh…and she had long fangs. I think that was what threw the image off so drastically, because they did not look like the mouth could contain them. And if they curled inwards when she shut her mouth, I would have to guess that they would come out the back of her head. The only way that I could make sense of them was to realize that my own Sharkmouth probably came across the same way. So, using that logic, I had to think that she invoked those fangs when she was about to feed.

That would bring me to the small child she had dangling by the ankle in her left hand. The little girl was probably six years old. She was wearing Elmo pajamas. Her face was a mask of horror as she looked down the throat of the lamia that was ready to make a meal of her.

I was about to close the distance between us when Butt Pimple tugged at my head and turned it sharply left. It was the grizzly exhibit. Sprawled on the rock ledge were Lisa and Nose Wart. Emerging from its cave was the large inhabitant. They were both just lying there.

"Poisoned!" Butt Pimple whispered.

My eyes narrowed and I could see two distinct punctures on Lisa and Nose Wart's throat. I looked back at the lamia as its mouth curled into an evil smile.

"Tick-tock, bitch!" the lamia hissed. Her voice was every bit that of what you would expect from a serpent.

I was faced with a choice. In one leap, I could be on the lamia…or in the bear exhibit. I cursed my exceptional ghoul eyesight as I could see the terror on Nose Wart's face and the tears streaming down Lisa's cheeks, her eyes wide as she stared at me.

I looked back at the lamia and saw her mouth going through some sort of transformation. It was widening and the jaw was unhinging. If my Sharkmouth looked anything like that, no wonder Lisa didn't want to be around me when I fed.

Almost as a taunt, the lamia jiggled the little girl that was now hovering over that grotesque mouth. I knew then that it was a choice. I could save one, but not all. If I jumped into the grizzly exhibit, I could fend the massive beast off and rescue Lisa as well as Nose Wart. Or, I could attack the lamia and keep her from eating the child.

But could I?

Lisa had said that the lamia had no known weakness. I had to make a choice. It ripped through me and made me realize that, while I may no longer be human, I was more than capable of having those good old mortal emotions. My heart broke as I leapt into the grizzly exhibit and scooped up Lisa and Nose Wart.

I no sooner landed when I heard a shriek of pain, horror, and something else. Betrayal. That was what my mind registered it as when that child let loose with such an agonizing sound.

With Lisa under one arm, Nose Wart under the other, and Butt Pimple still on my shoulders hanging on for dear life, I sprung from the rock ledge and landed in the grass across from the grizzly's little viewing area.

The lamia was making an over-exaggerated swallow as the child disappeared down her gullet. Dropping Lisa and Nose Wart, I launched myself at the monster, but with amazing speed, it slithered into the nearby woods.

Breathing deep, I made a point of committing the smell of this creature to memory. There was a nasty bitterness and a hint of sugary sweetness at the same time. The closest I can pin it to is Nyquil. Sorry, that is the best I have.

I stood at the edge of the grass and scanned the dense woods. The sounds of maniacal laughter began to fade, and I fought the urge to charge in after the creature. The only things preventing me were the defenseless bodies of Lisa and Nose Wart.

Butt Pimple was scrambling off my shoulders as I stood there stewing in my anger. I willed my fingers and toes back to normal when a voice shattered my heart.

"What in the hell is wrong with you!" Lisa screamed from behind me.

That Ghoul Ava…On the Lam!

5

Take Me Home Tonight

"Excuse me?" I turned to see Lisa on her hands and knees.

"You let that thing eat that poor child!" Lisa managed through tears. "Why would you do that? Are you really that divorced from humanity that you could allow something like that to happen while you did nothing!"

"Nothing?" I pointed to where she and Nose Wart were struggling to their feet, both staggering like drunks. "I saved *your* ass!"

Seriously? Did I need to point that out? And if she wanted me to feel bad, I had that handled without any help, thank you very much.

"At the cost of the life of an innocent child!" Lisa took a step towards me and then promptly fell back to the ground on her hands and knees where she began to wretch violently. And not just Lisa, Nose Wart was heaving just a few feet away while Butt Pimple stood over him wringing her hands in worry.

"It is the poison," the female goblin gurgled. "Their systems are now purging themselves."

I had sort of figured that out for myself, but it was good to get confirmation. I went to Lisa and knelt beside her, pulling her hair back. How many times had I done this with other cocktail waitresses or bartenders? She heaved and hurled for a while, but as soon as she was able, she jerked away from me.

"You should have saved that child," she spat.

"And let you and Nose Wart be mauled and probably killed by a grizzly bear?" I glanced over to see the massive beast still regarding us like maybe he (or she) hoped that his snack would once more be deposited in his habitat or whatever zoo people called those little areas where they tried to make themselves feel good about keeping a wild animal in a cage.

No, I am not some sort of animal activist, but I know well enough that wild animals are not like dogs or cats. Well...mostly dogs, but that is beside the point. Lions and tigers and bears (did you just say "Oh my!"?) probably do not like being kept in a zoo versus being able to run around in the woods or jungles.

"I am a Templar," Lisa said like that was all that she needed to say on the subject. When I just stared at her, she did me the *favor* of continuing on her little tirade. "We are trained and taught that we will give our lives in our duty if need be in order to preserve human life."

"Well excuse me for acting on my gut versus some ridiculous Templar code or logic." I turned and stared back towards the exit of the zoo.

I was almost to the gate when Nose Wart and Butt Pimple caught up. I did not look over my shoulder, because my senses told me what I did not want to actually confirm with my eyes. Lisa was not coming.

For crying out loud, can't we just go back to the way things were before this Templar nonsense?

"I apologize, Just Ava," Nose Wart groveled.

I spun on the goblin and fixed him with my jet black eyes. Predictably, he dropped to the ground on his belly and prostrated himself before me. His mate did likewise, both pleading for mercy.

"Oh get up!" I snapped. "Where did Lisa run off to?"

"She said that she will meet you at home later," a voice said from above me. It was a coarse, rough voice. It reminded me of boulders grinding together. I spun around to discover nothing.

"Up here, Ava the Ghoul," the voice called.

I looked up on top of the ticket booth and saw a large lump of darkness. That was strange since I have perfect night vision. Yet, for some reason, I could see nothing but a misshapen lump of black. Well, until the creature unfurled its wings.

I took an involuntary step back and I heard Nose Wart emit a frightened squeak. So much for goblins being fearless.

"And you are?" I took a step back and allowed my fingers to go all Wolverine (or Freddy Krueger if you prefer, but I assume that you get the idea).

"I do not have a name that would make sense to your ears." The creature rose up from the roof and then settled on the ground about ten feet from me.

"Oh…" Nose Wart gasped and scrambled to his feet. "It is one of the gargoyles."

The creature took a small hop forward and came to rest in a circle of light made brighter by the snow. In all honesty, I would have sworn it was a statue. It looked like something that was ripped from the eaves of a building. There were even a few cracks and what I am pretty sure had to be a bit of mossy growth in some of the folds.

At just about four feet high, it had a face that looked part human and part…lizard? The eyes were big saucers that swirled with flecks of copper and silver but had no real pupil that I could see. The feet were massive and tipped with hooked talons. As for the wings, I swear that they had the same stone-like appearance as the rest of the gargoyle, but they rippled and folded when the creature shifted them.

"Well I can't just call you Gargoyle. So how about Rex?"

The gargoyle tilted its head one way and then the other much like a puppy. It hopped towards me, and I had to do my best not to react. I had no idea what this thing's intentions might be, but I was hoping that they were not aggressive.

"I will accept being called Rex," the gargoyle replied with a rattling sound that I was going to classify as a chuckle. Rex narrowed his eyes and returned to business. "I am one of the servants of the Templar, Lisa Jenkins."

Wait. Lisa had servants? When did this happen? We were

absolutely going to have a talk when she got home. She might be a Templar, and I might not be her parent, but...what? Did I have any claim or right to know anything? If she was just a roommate, would she be required to tell me every little thing? Still, a gargoyle servant?

"And you said that she will meet me at home later?" I asked. While I was relaxing just a bit, I had not reached a point where I was willing to retract my claws. Just because this thing threw Lisa's name around did not make us friends or even polite acquaintances.

"She has left with my mate," Rex answered with a ruffling of his wings—at least I think it is a he. How do you tell with a gargoyle?

"And you are the one who brought her here?" I asked.

"I am."

"You brought her here to try and fight a lamia?"

"I merely did as I was told." That was a simple enough answer. I wish that my minions were as subservient as this thing seemed to be when it came to obeying Lisa's commands.

"And can you take her a message for me?" I asked.

"I am sorry, Ava the Ghoul. I cannot do that thing. My service is to Lisa and her alone."

I pursed my lips, once again wishing that my little band of misfit miscreants were so dialed in to me. I tried to picture Nose Wart refusing to do something that Morgan requested and sighed.

"Okay, well, I guess we are done here," I said with a shrug.

"Actually, I am to follow you home and await Lisa's return," Rex said, hopping twice before becoming airborne. With a few flaps of his massive leathery wings (that still looked like stone to me) he was back on top of the ticket booth.

"Can I ask you another question?" I called over my shoulder as I scooped up Nose Wart and Butt Pimple.

"You may ask as many questions as you wish, Ava the Ghoul."

"Why can't I see you? My vision is perfect in the dark, but when I look at you, unless you step out into the light, all I see is—"

"I am not fully formed in this…*dimension* is the best word to your understanding," Rex cut me off with his explanation.

I would ask Morgan next time we met up. I was not sure what the gargoyle meant by dimension, and I was not prepared to ask and display my ignorance to yet another creature of the Supernatural community. Like my granddaddy used to say, "Better to keep your mouth shut and be thought the fool than to open it and remove all doubt."

I climbed back in the truck and held up a silencing finger when Aoife looked like she was going to say something.

I did not want to recount what had happened with the lamia, I did not want to talk about Lisa, and I did not want to talk about gargoyles from other dimensions. I just wanted to go home.

That Ghoul Ava…On the Lam!

6

Love is a Battlefield

"You let another child die!" Morgan said with her usual lack of emotion, Yet, I swear that I could hear anger and even more disapproval than normal in her tone.

"Did you miss the part about Lisa being served up as Grizzly Chow?" I was really trying to keep my emotions in check. I knew that if I let go, I might explode. I was already churning with guilt over the death of that child. I'd had Lisa give me a ration about it, and now Morgan.

"Without the knowledge of the Templar's, she might have lost on both fronts."

I am pretty sure my jaw bounced off the floor. The very last person that I expected any sort of support from, no matter how slight or even unintentional, was from Belinda. Yet there she was, in short shorts and a bare midriff tee shirt emblazoned with the picture of some band called One Republic.

Maybe this was a reward for not mentioning her wardrobe when she and Morgan had arrived just after sunset. The temperature could not be above twenty degrees and there was a good six or seven inches of snow on the ground, but I had kept my mouth shut about her outfit. Seriously, she is a vampire, it is not like she was going to die from exposure…unless that exposure was to the sun.

"That is beside the point. She was tasked to stop these child murders. Have you seen the news today?" Morgan accepted the cup of tea from Aoife and blew across the surface before taking a sip.

I had to admit, I still had not made any effort to watch the local news. I hated how they all just carried on *ad nauseum* whenever they got their hooks into a story. The more terrible the story, the more it was driven into the ground by the television talking heads.

"No," I said needlessly. Morgan probably already knew the answer. No doubt she was just trying to drive her point home.

"This time the child was the only daughter of a city commissioner," Morgan informed me.

"So?" I shot back.

"What do you mean *so?*"

Wow, Morgan actually sounded noticeably angry. I was really under her skin; either that, or perhaps this case was more important than I was realizing. Still, I had a point to make as well, and she just opened the door for me to do so.

"What makes that child any more important than the others? Just because it is the child of some politician, does that make her life worth more than the others? That is why I don't watch televised news. They have a screwed up sense of priority. Some celebrity gets a hang nail and we got doctors giving helpful hints on how to keep from having such a terrible malady happen to us "normal" folks. I got news for you, every single one of the children who died has left behind a family that is devastated and grieving."

"Of course," Morgan agreed. I was suddenly wary. Her voice was back to being calm. That, and she had just agreed with me…sort of. "I am not saying that any one child is more or less important than another. What I am saying is that this gains more public exposure now, and if the humans discover us, there could be dire consequences."

"Maybe we are underestimating this," I offered. "Have you seen all the crap people read based on our reality? And the television is overloaded with weres, vamps, and zombies. Humans might actually be ready to accept us."

"That is the real fiction." Morgan shook her head. "Monsters on the screen or the page are one thing, but in real life?"

"We already tried that once a few hundred years ago," Aoife added. "That is where so much of what humans now refer to as mythology comes from. We were hunted down to the point of near extinction."

"That was then," I retorted. "Things have changed. Heck, I remember when it used to be illegal for mixed marriages to take place. Granted, I was really young—"

"It is not going to happen, so stop wasting time with this ridiculous argument!" Morgan snapped.

The entire room went silent. Even more surprising, Belinda actually got up and just left. Not a word to anybody, she simply walked out and shut the door behind her.

"Fine." I threw my hands up in a sign of surrender. "But you still have not answered my question."

"Which question is that?" Morgan said after another sip of her tea.

"Gargoyles?" I did not feel the need to elaborate. She knew what I meant.

"Yes." Morgan gave a sage nod. "And our Miss Lisa has apparently attracted a pair so you say."

"I guess. I mean, the one that stayed behind—" I started, but Aoife's laughing cut me off. I turned her direction with a severe expression. She covered her mouth, but the giggling continued. "What is wrong with the name Rex?" I challenged.

"Nothing is wrong with it," Aoife finally managed. "I just cannot imagine a gargoyle allowing such a thing."

"Yes," Morgan spoke, "but be that as it may, you say that there were two? You are certain? And one said that they were a mated pair?"

"Yeah." Pretty straight forward stuff as far as I was concerned. Personally, I think Morgan was stalling while she decided what to tell me and what to keep to herself.

"First, the word dimension is not accurate. The gargoyles exist on another plane from mortals. According to legend, they were summoned through by a powerful earth witch. However, her magic was not quite strong enough to bring them all the way through. This was both a blessing and a curse for the gargoyle. If they are slain on this plane of existence, they are actually just returned to their own. Unfortunately, that is also the only way that they can return home. The reason that you don't see them in the conventional sense is because they don't fully exist here."

That was as good of an explanation as any, I guess. But she only answered part of my question. The rest of it had to do with why these two were supposedly bonded with Lisa or whatever it is that gargoyles do when they commit to serve a Templar.

"I have no earthly idea why they are attached to the girl," Morgan finally said.

It took me a few seconds, but then I realized why she had been so hesitant to answer that part of my question. It meant admitting that she did not know something!

"She was supposedly coming home after whatever it was that she had to slip away for." That admission made me grumpy. It just felt like every single time Lisa and I started to close the gap that was between us, something would come along and tear it back open again.

Almost as if on cue, the front door opened and in she walked. After stomping the snow from her boots, Lisa hung up her coat and strolled into the living room. I was trying to decide what my approach would be this time, but fortunately, Morgan spoke up.

"Perhaps you might let people know when you are just going to disappear for a day in the clutches of a gargoyle."

"First," Lisa turned to Morgan, "I would have expected that from *her*." She hiked a thumb over her shoulder to where I stood in the doorway to the kitchen. "And second, I am an adult. I do not owe anybody an accounting of my whereabouts."

"Excuse me?" Morgan said, the slightest tick of one corner of her mouth the only indication of emotion. "First off, Miss Jenkins, you might be what is currently defined by society as an adult, but your actions would argue against such points."

Holy crap! Morgan used air quotes. This was going to be a

good ass chewing.

"And second, adult or child, there is a thing called courtesy. Gargoyle or no, this up and vanishing is unacceptable. Whatever your leanings may be, you are now a member of the Templars. If Ava is your friend as you *claim*, then this constant disappearing by you says otherwise." Lisa opened her mouth, but Morgan was not finished. "And *third*, you conscript gargoyles and do not think to let anybody else know?"

It was like watching a fish that had been yanked out of the water and tossed on the shore. Lisa's mouth opened and shut a dozen times, but no sound came out. At last, she dropped her head. After a deep breath, she looked up. I was half-expecting an angry expression. What I was not expecting was the flush of shame or embarrassment that had crept up her cheeks.

"Ava," she turned to me, "I am sorry. I had no right tearing into you last night and then just taking off. I could see on your face how much the death of that child hit you. I was just frustrated. Morgan is right. You are my friend. I tell you over and over that I would never turn on you, but my actions have probably done nothing to convince you of my sincerity."

"Well," I shrugged, "I think we can both admit that things have been a bit crazy."

"Regardless," Lisa shook her head, "that doesn't give me the right to treat you the way that I have been treating you. In the end, all we have is each other." A tear welled up and trickled down Lisa's cheek.

The next thing I knew, we were hugging each other and she was balling her eyes out. A second later, Aoife was in the mix as well and a lot Kleenex ended up on the floor. At least that was where it was dropped. Somehow, it all ended up gone by the time eyes were dry and everybody was back to normal. I thought I saw a few of the goblins scurrying around underfoot, but I chose to let that part of what was otherwise a beautiful moment just slip away.

"Are we done?" Leave it to Morgan to harsh everybody's mellow.

"Actually, no." Lisa surprised me by speaking. I am pretty

sure that Morgan had tossed that out as a rhetorical question. "I have a few things to say and share about the lamia."

7

Round and Round

"She can be killed."

That was a good start. I gave Lisa's hand one more squeeze and then sat down in the recliner. Morgan was on the loveseat, and I didn't feel that we were at a point where either of us would be comfortable cozying up together. And as for the couch, it was suddenly filled with a good dozen goblins. Aoife took my spot standing in the entry to the kitchen and now all eyes were focused on Lisa.

"There is a potion that can be made. But the catch comes in the ingredients. They all have to be gathered within three hours of use and the witch who creates the potion has to be present to utter the final phrase as the potion is sprinkled on the lamia."

I shot a look at Aoife, but she was locked on to Lisa with every bit of her attention. Her face had not even twitched when Lisa mentioned a witch needing to be involved.

"And what are the ingredients?" Morgan asked the million dollar question.

"Okay, here is where I have a problem," Lisa sighed. "If these are literal, I don't know where we can come up with them, much less within three hours."

"Just tell us what they are," I urged. "I think I know somebody who can answer the questions about if these are literal

61

items or figurative ones."

"Twin baby tears, a new mother's first milk, nightshade, and ground silver mixed with ash made from the callouses of a new father's hands." Lisa looked around the room. "There are few assorted herbs and such that seem pretty normal, but those first four items are more than a bit strange."

"I can assure you that they are quite literal," Morgan said at last. "And if you think about them, they make perfect sense."

I thought about them, but they still just seemed weird. Where was the eye of newt or toe of frog? Of course my prior experience with witches were Samantha from *Bewitched* and that little blond from *Sabrina the Teenage Witch*. And NO! I am not talking about that gawdawful show with that Melissa Joan Hart tramp. I am talking about the really bitchin' cartoon from my childhood with the Groovie Ghoulies. And if you don't know what I am talking about, you have my pity.

"Let me call somebody." I pulled out my phone.

"No need," Morgan said with a shake of her head. "I have a witch that excels in potions."

"Fine." Maybe this was for the best.

I was actually relieved. After that little tiff that Aoife had over Rosanna, I was not sure if that particular witch would be all that interested in returning to my house. What I needed to do now was get Aoife to make herself scarce.

I got up and made for the kitchen as Morgan made her call. I pointed at the siren and indicated that she duck back into the kitchen as well so that we could talk in private. I opened the door to the basement and ushered her in and down the stairs.

"Yes, miss?" Aoife said with genuine curiosity. I had a hard time believing that she was not aware why I was pulling her aside.

"We will be working with a witch." That should do it.

"I know that, miss. I heard all that Miss Jenkins said on the matter." Aoife still sounded like nothing in the world might be wrong.

Had I missed something? She'd told me all about the reason why sirens hated witches. Heck, I even saw the reason as logical and with some degree of merit. Were there different types of witches? Was that the deal?

"So you need to sit this one out. Maybe stay here at the house?" I offered.

"I think I should be with you on this one, miss. In fact, I believe that you should bring the bugbears as well…and perhaps all the goblins. They might serve as suitable distractions in this fight."

I did not want to know what Aoife meant when she referred to the goblins as being distractions in this little adventure. As much as I hated to admit it, I'd grown fond of the ugly, stinky little creatures with their quasi-offensive sounding names and propensity to spit when angry. I could no more sacrifice one of them as I could a cute and cuddly puppy…or an ugly one for that matter.

The best way to describe the allure (for lack of a better word) of the goblin, is to compare them to English Bulldogs. They are simply an ugly dog. But they are so ugly that they are absolutely adorable. And I knew a few bulldog owners; they are almost famous for their flatulence. Seriously, they have to be cute to keep their owners from tossing them out of the car in the middle of nowhere. And before you even think for a second that I am a monster for suggesting such a thing, that last line was a quote from a bulldog owner that loved that breed more than her own children.

"But there will be a witch on this little trip," I reminded. Actually, I did not think that I needed to remind her. She is as smart as she is pretty. I think I was simply stating it out loud so that I could watch her reaction.

"Yes, miss. And I do not dispute their functionality."

"So you won't be grabbing this one around the throat when she arrives?"

"No, miss. There is a greater evil to tend to. And who knows, maybe she will be a fatality on the mission. There is always hope."

With that, the siren simply walked out of the kitchen. I swear, my jaw was gonna sprain itself if it dropped open any more tonight.

I walked out into the living room to discover Morgan quietly sipping her tea and the goblins all staring at her like she was doing something amazing. Aoife and Lisa were both absent. That gave me a few seconds alone with the Psychic. For what it was worth, I was going to bounce a few questions off her in the hopes that she might spill something meaningful in her half-answers.

"Did you know that sirens and witches hate each other?" That seemed as good of a place to start as any.

"With good reason," Morgan answered with the slightest lift and drop of her shoulders that might have been a shrug.

"Should I keep an eye on this witch of yours and Aoife?"

"You need to keep your focus on the lamia. Of all the individuals that need to walk back through that front door when this is over, you are primary."

"Wow...didn't know that you cared?" I snarked, plopping down in the recliner.

"Ava, we can do this some other time. You need to get your mind on the task at hand. There is a very dangerous creature out there, and she has struck again."

"What!" I exclaimed. "How do you know?"

Morgan pointed to the muted television where a reporter was standing in front of a non-descript house on a dark street. The caption underneath read: *Serial Killer Strikes Again!*

"So how is this getting to the news so quickly?" I asked. "If the child just came up missing, how do they know it is their supposed serial killer?"

"You really haven't paid any attention to the news, have you?" Morgan asked, setting her tea cup down. When I shook my head, she sighed and closed her eyes, pinching the bridge of her nose. "The clothes." That was all Morgan said, so why did I feel a chill wind whip up in the depths of my soul?

"What about them?" Something told me that I really did not want to know.

"The ripped and bloody remnants of their clothing are left on the doorstep."

I have no idea how long I stood there in stunned silence. Once I was able to recover from that punch in the gut, I asked what I thought to be the obvious question. "How is this creature getting in to town to these residences to leave the clothing without somebody being able to detect her?"

Morgan's eyes shifted just slightly, but I saw very clearly her answer. I looked over at the goblins that were now busy passing something around that looked like a yacked up hairball.

"You think that this lamia…" I left the question open.

"She is not alone."

I saw how that might be a problem. What I did not see or understand was why it had Morgan so apparently upset.

"You are gonna have to do better than that," I finally said.

"If she was sent here, then she has managed to overcome the dread that would eventually consume her. That also means that she is not acting on impulse, but rather from sheer and complete malice."

That was a lot to take in, but I was not about to bitch. Morgan was not known for telling me that much. If she was spilling the beans like this, then there had to be a reason. I was just about to blurt out Claude's name as the suspect when Morgan fixed me with a hard stare.

"This could be an attempt by the council to remove me from my post," Morgan said in a voice that was soft enough that I am certain I was the only one who could hear.

I was about to ask why when the knock came at the front door. Much like dogs, all the goblins jumped off the couch and rushed down the entry hall in a cacophony of grunts, squeaks, and yes, barks. I briefly wondered if I might be able to grab some dog food from the store instead of feeding these little walking stomachs the cauldrons of pasta and other such things I had been giving them since their arrival.

When I opened the door, I was surprised to see Rosanna standing there. She was wearing the cutest pink ski jacket and some really expensive looking boots. She also had a large knapsack slung over her shoulder.

"Umm…" Yeah that was the best I could do.

"Morgan called for me." Rosanna gave a little dip of her head as if asking me to invite her in. I stepped aside and welcomed her.

"I didn't know that you worked for Morgan," I said as I took her coat and hung it up.

"Where is your kitchen?" Rosanna asked almost absently. She took a few steps and then paused, turning to me with an embarrassed grin. "Sorry, I am just running through everything that I need to do for this spell and am a little pre-occupied."

"No problem, I understand." I really didn't. Unless that was how I came across when I spaced out, then I had to wonder how people did not just absolutely hate me.

We headed for the kitchen where Aoife was sitting on a counter as if waiting for us. Now, the reason *that* is worth noting is because she is not the sit-on-the-counter type. She is much too formal and reserved for something so very casual. If Rosanna noticed, she said nothing.

Instead, she went to the table and set down her knapsack. I moved aside as Morgan came in with a gaggle of goblins on her heels. The only person missing was Lisa, and that was quickly remedied as my friend came in through the backside entrance to the kitchen. That was when the entire room seemed to freeze. Seriously, I actually glanced at Rosanna to see if perhaps she had cast that same spell from the other night. Nope. She was staring at Lisa just like everybody else.

"What?" Lisa asked, sounding very self-conscious.

"You want to explain?" Morgan asked before I could.

Lisa was dressed like a cross between a medieval warlord and a fetish queen. She had a studded leather corset, fine chain gloves that went to the elbows, a spiked collar—and by spiked, I mean these things were easily two or three inches long and looked like they would cause serious harm. In fact, I was willing to bet that they would punch a hole in Lisa if she moved her head suddenly in a downward direction. Her legs were wrapped in what looked like leather with metal fibers that I was guessing to be silver woven throughout. The belt she wore had a dozen weapons hanging from it, only a few that resembled anything that I had ever seen before, the highlight being the long, curved blade. Oh, and she had another much larger sword poking up from behind one shoulder.

"Do I need to?" Lisa asked, dismissing Morgan's comment as she walked in and leaned against the back door, arms folded across her chest (that was really being accented by that leather corset thing in a way that I was actually almost jealous of) with a look of grim determination etched on her face.

"I may be alone, but I'm gonna go with yes," I said with a gesture at her outfit.

"This is my Templar battle gear," Lisa said with a shrug.

"I know what it is," Morgan said with a shake of her head. "I mean how is it that you already have this? I thought you did not receive your full attire until your training was complete."

With a sigh, Lisa held up one hand and plucked the gauntlet from it one finger at a time. There, on her wedding finger was a ring with a black and white stone.

"Since when?" Morgan asked.

"Since shortly after the decree for Ava's capture and execution was announced," Lisa replied.

"Wait…what?" I sputtered.

"Can we do this later?" Rosanna almost hollered.

All eyes turned to her. She had a few jars and pouches laid out before her along with a brass pot that looked like a miniature replica of the stereotypical witch's cauldron.

"I need to concentrate to work this magic."

That Ghoul Ava…On the Lam!

8

Magic

The room grew silent and the goblins scurried out of the kitchen, yelping like they'd been kicked or something. Rosanna had the sudden realization of just who she had screamed at and turned a deep crimson.

"Sorry," she squeaked. "It's just that I can't get this wrong. I have just enough of each of the trigger components to create this one time. If I screw this up, we might have to wait a couple of weeks for a few of these items to be gathered again."

I was not going to ask where or how she came upon *any* of these items. I mean, who gathers baby tears…much less from twins? And that was just one of the items. A mother's first milk? Gross!

Rosanna bent over her items and began humming as she added one thing after another to the copper cauldron. Lisa and I were captivated. Morgan seemed disinterested, and Aoife was picking at her nails in another display of very uncharacteristic behavior.

After lighting a red candle that smelled like vomit and putting the cauldron on some sort of stand over the flame, she began to mutter in a language that was absolutely not English (I would guess at Latin, but it would just be a guess). Moments later, a fog began to rise from my floor. I seemed to be the only person bothered by it, so I just stayed quiet and pretended that everything was hunky dory.

The lights flickered a few times, but that could just be the old house combined with the winds whipping up outside. I glanced out the kitchen window and saw snow swirling up from the ground in a dozen little snow cyclones. Having never been around an actual witch, I had to admit that this was in reality a lot cooler than her just twitching her nose.

I was actually really excited. I had never seen a witch do anything before, and this was so much cooler than I expected. And if I was interested, Lisa was practically hypnotized by what was happening.

I heard a moaning sound and my eyes darted back to the cauldron. A swirl of ugly grayish smoke swirled up and became an even uglier greenish color. It was a lamia! I watched the smoke as it wafted upwards and the smoke-lamia seemed to rise up and writhe around the edge of the cauldron.

"Whoa!" I breathed.

That earned a sharp look from Morgan, and I quickly did a "button the lip" gesture, being sure to throw away the key. The goblins all crept back in and began to form a circle around the table. I was not sure if it was so that they could all see, or if they were actually creating some sort of protective barricade.

"It is ready," Rosanna finally said in a hitching gasp like she had just finished running a thousand yard dash.

I glanced at Morgan, but she simply nodded at me. Tentatively, I stepped forward and opened my hand to accept the tiny vial. It was warm to the touch, and when I held it up to the light, I could see something swirling around inside of it. I was suddenly hit with a peculiar feeling of sadness.

"So, what do I do?" I asked. I had to suppress a shiver that tried to ripple through me.

Rosanna gulped a few more times, and I noticed a sheen of perspiration on her face. *Wow*, I thought, *magic is a lot more difficult in real life than it is in the movies and on television.*

"You have to pour it down her throat," Rosanna finally managed.

"Excuse me?" I blurted. *I might as well just cut her head off while I'm at it*. I kept that last bit to myself, but I am pretty sure my tone said it all.

"You did not think that this was going to be easy, did you?" Morgan sniffed.

"Well, maybe not easy, but I was hoping to catch at least a bit of a break."

"Don't worry, Ava," Lisa offered. "You will have plenty of support."

"Umm," I started, but was hesitant to ask the question poking up in my mind. I could not deny the feeling that had sunk in as soon as she had handed me the potion and it was annoyingly constant.

Rosanna squeaked and snatched the potion back. "You've hand an affair with a married man." She did not say it as an accusation, more like she was reciting a fact.

I nodded, making a very conscious effort to not look directly at either Morgan or Lisa. I did not need to see their faces to know the judgment that was certainly in their eyes. Hey, I wasn't proud of it…and it was a one-time thing that I made a point not to repeat ever again.

"This is a very potent concoction," Rosanna finally explained. "When you give this to the lamia, her guilt will actually consume her from the inside out. From what I have been told, it will look sort of like a deflating balloon until there is nothing left but the shell."

"The shell?" I asked, trying to shift the subject away from just another regrettable moment from my past.

"Like a shed snake skin."

"Gross," I gasped.

"And if it is not too much trouble," Rosanna added sheepishly, "could I have those remains?"

"Why?" I didn't actually have a problem with it, but I could not deny being curious.

"Magic properties," Morgan answered for the witch. "There are undoubtedly a myriad of uses for such a rare item."

"I don't see any problems with that." I shrugged my shoulders. I felt Blodwen stir somewhere in my head, but when she remained silent, I dismissed it as perhaps my guilty conscience.

There was another sudden and familiar pattering of tiny feet and the goblins, who had been all but forgotten the past few minutes, all scurried away from the table, gathering in front of me. Nose Wart stepped forward and bowed low like he was in some sort of royal court presenting himself to the queen.

"We will not fail you, Just Ava." He stood, and I noticed a gleam in his eyes that I'd never seen before. "We shall place our lives on the table and offer them willingly if that is what must be done to ensure that you are victorious."

A rumbling from behind me caused me to turn and I saw the bugbears gathered in my living room. One of them stepped forward and nodded. That was all, but their message was clear.

You have gathered yourself quite an army, Blodwen spoke from somewhere deep in my mind.

It had been a while since I'd heard any of the "voices" in my head. I'd almost forgotten about them. With Adrianna locked away, I was amazed at the amount of peace that existed in me.

I do not have an army, I insisted, but it was a weak denial at best. Almost as if to mock that thought, a dull thud came from the wall of my kitchen. Outside the same window that I'd seen the snow cyclones a moment ago, the fiery jötunn were hunched down and staring in at me. *Okay, maybe a platoon, but not an army*.

"So, when do we go?" Lisa asked, snapping me back to the situation at hand.

"No time like the present," I said with a shrug.

"What about them?" she hiked a thumb over her shoulder at the huge faces smooshed together and staring in from outside.

"Good point." I walked over to the window and cracked it open. "You kids need to stay here and protect the house."

There was a low grumble of discontent, but it was Lisa who came to the rescue. "You need to keep those massive hounds from returning to the yard and leaving their mess."

I was actually surprised when the young giants all nodded vigorously. A thought came to me and I stepped up beside Lisa.

"No eating the dogs." Their crestfallen expressions told me all I needed to know.

"How did you know?" Lisa whispered as we all headed out to the truck.

"I didn't," I replied with a shrug.

I paused when I noticed one of us was missing. I turned to see Morgan standing in the door to the house.

"I take it you are staying behind to help the giants?" I quipped.

"You should know better than that." And then she shut the door.

It took some jostling. When Aoife went to climb in back with the menagerie already sort of crammed in the bed of the truck, I pulled her aside. "You sure you are okay?"

"I am fine, miss."

Something did not sit right with me on this one. I wish that I was better at reading people. Or sirens as the current case may be.

"Would you tell me otherwise?"

She smiled and hopped in with the goblins and bugbears who seemed even more surprised than I was at the newest occupant to join them in the back of the pickup. I didn't have time for this, so I went to the cab, climbed in and headed for my date with the lamia.

That Ghoul Ava…On the Lam!

9

U Got the Look

The parking lot in front of the Portland Zoo looked like pretty much any other parking lot after a nice snowfall. By that, I mean gross. There were tracks and trails everywhere as people mindlessly destroyed the pristine white beauty that snow brings. I even spotted a few huge circles where somebody decided to whip their car around in donuts. I never understood that fascination.

Yeah, I am one of those people who hated building a snowman in her yard. I would rather look outside and see the untouched white. Just a personal preference.

I pulled in to a parking space and shut off the truck. I had noticed a seriousness in Lisa during the drive that actually sort of gave me the creeps. Her lips were pressed tight and her eyes looked absolutely devoid of any emotion. That is not something that looks normal on a teenage girl. Not unless she was one of the Manson Family.

As I stepped out into the hard and jagged snow that was quickly freezing into a solid sheet as the temperature continued to drop and the wind kicked up to furious gusts that made me glad I was not a warm bodied creature subject to the harshness that I knew such things brought.

The tailgate to the truck dropped and the goblins spilled out with the bugbears. The last to emerge was Aoife. She did not look the least bit ruffled. I was about to say something when a set of headlights turned in to the massive open lot. There was a pause, and then the headlights turned our direction.

"Crap, it's the cops," I snarled.

For just a moment I was hit with a dose of concern. I was standing in the open with a bunch of goblins, some bugbears, a siren, a witch, and a Templar. It sounded like the start to a bad joke.

The squad car angled just enough to present a broadside of the vehicle. The driver's side window rolled down.

"A nasty night out," the officer said, his eyes scanning my little band.

"Yeah," I said with a slow drawl that made that single word last much too long.

"Here for a special photo shoot," Lisa's voice piped up as she came up beside me.

I saw the officer's eyes scan the girl, pausing at each weapon and taking an extremely inappropriate pause at her bunched up boobies courtesy of the corset. Uniform or not, this guy was an actual pig.

"Those look mighty dangerous, missy," the officer said with more than just a little condescension in his voice.

"These old things?" Lisa laughed. "Most of them would break if I swung at an icicle."

The officer seemed to consider her words. He glanced at the bugbears and then back to me. "Some pretty impressive makeup."

"Yes, we work with a television show that is filmed here," Lisa continued.

Now, I instantly knew what show she was referring to and had to give her seriously mad props for coming up with this stuff on the fly. However, the cop did not seem to know what she was talking about and gave her comment a dismissive wave.

"Just be careful. You might die of exposure dressed that way." He actually gave her a wink!

I wanted to reach in that window and yank him out by his

fat face. (Okay, it wasn't actually fat, but you get the point.) I was about to try and excuse ourselves so we could get on with what we came for when a few of the goblins decided that they wanted to climb up on the squad car's hood!

Before I could shoo them off, Aoife poked me in the ribs. I turned and saw her very slightly shake her head. It took me a few seconds to realize…the cop couldn't see them! For regular humans (and for reasons that I make no claim to understand) goblins are basically invisible to the human eye. Lisa could see them because she was special. In fact, it had been Morgan who told me that the girl was tuned in and might even express some limited powers as a Psychic.

"We do need to get moving, officer," Lisa said with the absolute most fake smile that I had ever seen. Seriously, how do men not pick up on that? We do it all the time, but if you add a little batting of the eyelashes, they are absolute simpletons.

The squad car pulled away in a crunch of tires carving their way through the ice-crusted snow. I wasn't surprised that he didn't stick to the ruts created by the day's traffic. Instead, it was like he made it a point to cut through as much of the very little remaining untouched patches of the beautiful white blanket as he could manage.

At last, his tail lights vanished around the corner and he was gone. I turned to Lisa. "Good work!"

"You sound so surprised," Lisa snorted as she drew the curved blade at her hip. "Now, can we get this done and get home. Templars did not design these outfits for the cold."

I glanced at her leather corset and the expanse of bare skin between the décolletage that shoved Lisa's cleavage up like some sick parody of a teen sword-and-sorcery fantasy and that spiked collar. I was just the teensiest bit jealous. It was a very sexy outfit. Maybe I would "borrow" it sometime when she was not home or gone on some training mission.

The thing is, I had to admit that Lisa had handled that situation exceptionally well. She had known that man was gawking, so she used it to her advantage. She was growing up before my eyes, and in ways that I would have never imagined. And while I might be able to take some credit in the life I'd provided for her compared to the one she'd had, I also wondered what she was learning from the Templars.

As she walked away, I noticed that she did not simply walk. Nope, she had a sultry slink to her movements that screamed sexiness. She had gone from girl to a very hot young woman somewhere along the way. How had I missed that?

And then I realized something else. She was leading! She was not waiting for me or the goblins and bugbears. She was headed into battle, and we were following her.

We started for the entrance to the zoo. In a jiffy, I had boosted over everybody that needed help—by that, I mean Rosanna and the goblins—then, with me taking up the rear, I vaulted over and took a sniff. I had not realized it consciously, but the smell of the lamia was etched in my mind. I chalked it up to my forethought and planning when I'd made a point to catalog her smell during that first encounter.

"After confirming where Belinda saw the lamia, and then considering where Ava and I saw it, I am guessing that we should search the ravine that runs along the back side of the zoo," Lisa said.

I had to admit, Lisa certainly seemed to be running this operation. I wish I'd had my head that together when I was her age. Of course, there was the whole situation of where she was when I'd first met her. Maybe this was a case of me actually being a positive influence on the girl's life. And having met her mother once (sort of), it was clear that she'd not had much of a positive role model in her house.

Maybe you can pat yourself on the back later, Blodwen's voice interrupted my thoughts. *Right now, you need to keep all of your attention on dealing with this lamia. This is a nasty creature, and I think you will be needing all of your faculties about you.*

I hate it when the voice in my head makes a valid point.

We reached the trees and I made the group come to a stop. We would be tromping down this embankment in nasty conditions. I had my doubts as to whether or not I could navigate it without breaking my leg in the best of circumstances. These were *not* those conditions.

"Nose Wart, take a few of your fellow goblins and scout ahead. Hurry back if you see anything suspicious." Hey, what is the point in having minions if you don't use them?

"Right away, Just Ava!" Nose Wart did a snappy salute and pointed to a trio of his comrades.

I watched as they ducked into the thick evergreen wall. It was only a matter of moments before they came scurrying back out of the ravine. The chatter was so fast that it made my head hurt.

"Everybody be quiet!" I barked. The goblins all snapped their mouths shut with audible clicks. I pointed to Nose Wart. "Okay, you first. What did you see?"

"It is down there," Nose Wart said after taking a frightened glance over his shoulder. "And she has another ch—" The word was not out of his mouth when Lisa plunged into the woods and went bounding and crashing down the steep slope.

"Crap," I muttered, taking off after her. Hadn't she learned her lesson the last time she tried this little act of stupidity?

I was halfway down the slope when the flock of goblins went rocketing past, yelling, whooping, and making quite a racket. Well, so much for the element of surprise.

That Ghoul Ava…On the Lam!

10

For Whom the Bell Tolls

I reached the bottom and my feet plunged through a thin layer of ice that coated either a very small pond or a very large puddle. Besides not being subject to the elements and unbothered by the cold, the one good thing was that I could see the path of destruction that Lisa had made as she had stomped her way across and into an area thick with old, dead blackberry vines.

"Perhaps you should hurry after her," Aoife said as she slid to a graceful stop beside me.

That was probably a good idea. I could hear the goblins yipping and grunting in their guttural language. When had I been shuffled to the role of backup? Just a few short months ago, I was making Lisa hang back as I ventured forward into the newest version of the "Jaws of Death."

"I will be right behind you," Rosanna said with a pained hiss as the cold from this little puddle/pond hit her.

I glanced down at her feet and tsk'd at her choice of shoes. While I certainly love Nikes, this was not a good place for that sort of footwear. Maybe I would get her some proper boots for Christmas.

I took off after Lisa and the goblins. The bugbears fell in beside me, and one of them actually pushed ahead to tear through the briars and brambles. I would have to ask later if those sticker bushes hurt, but for now, I was following my sniffer. The lamia was close, and so was something else. Something hit my ghoul sense of smell. It was sweeter than candy. In a flash, I recalled the last time I'd smelt something so yummy.

"She has killed another child," I groaned.

And then we burst into a clearing. It was something out of a horror movie. A really *bad* horror movie. The clearing was littered with tiny piles of cracked and broken bones. The skulls were what gave it away. Much like I ralph up the clothes of those I ate in the early days before I learned that it was easier to simply undress the bodies, it seemed that the lamia could not digest the bones of her victims. The skulls, however, were the only things that had not suffered horrendous damage during consumption. The ribcages were a mess to the point where I had to wonder how they did not shred the lamia's insides on the way back up.

Lisa was kneeling beside something, and it took me a moment to process what I was seeing. Yes, I am a ghoul. I am a monster by definition. That did not make what I was seeing any easier to accept. I felt my anger reach a new level that I had not known could exist. For the briefest of milliseconds, I think I heard or felt Blodwen try to protest, and maybe Cody shrieked in horror. But my mind shut all of that out as I stepped up beside Lisa, the goblins gathered around her quickly scurried to get out of my way.

"I don't even have words," I gasped.

On the ground was a child. To be more accurate, the mangled remnants of half of a child. To add to this nightmare, it was the upper half. The face was frozen in an expression of the purest horror. I can't even begin to imagine what that poor thing saw to scare her so badly.

She could not have been older than five or six. Her dark hair was still in loose braids that were now starting to stiffen as the blood-soaked strands began to freeze. Her little pink top was desecrated with dark stains. One arm had been arranged and was pointing straight to the cave opening at the other side of the clearing. Almost too stereotypically, there was a pair of sputtering torches mounted on either side of the entrance.

I sniffed, and the realization was sudden…but also too late. All of our attention was on that dark cave. It could almost be considered an elaborate "Hey, look behind you!" gimmick. My sense told me, albeit a bit tardy, that the lamia was behind us.

The horrific creature burst from some nearby brush and slammed into Lisa. The blow caught her square in the middle of the back, resulting in a lung-emptying whoosh. Just that quick, the bold Templar was out of the fight.

I however, was not.

With a growl, I sprung and caught the lamia right where the upper, human-like torso melded into the serpent lower half. The two of us rolled twice, and I drove both clawed hands into the guts of this bitch.

Then I screamed.

Like the creatures from that movie *Alien*, it seemed that the blood of a lamia was acid. I felt the flesh from my hands literally start to melt from the bone. Leaping back, I glanced down and saw something that sent me scrambling for Ava Land. My left hand was nothing but a sick skeletal appendage. It belonged in a jar on display in a freak show.

Speaking of freak shows, for whatever reason, that is where my mind went as I blotted out the pain. Just a few days before all of this crap started, I had sat down to binge on the first seven episodes of *American Horror Story: Freak Show*. I was skimming through the episodes and trying to decide which were based on reality and which ones were made up.

Leaping up to the branch of an old pine tree, I split my mind—seriously, that is the best way to describe it. One part of it was wondering if the two-headed girl was alive or not, and the other was surveying the scene below.

The goblins had taken my cue and rushed in to attack. I saw three of them grappling with the tail of the lamia. It had a nasty looking stinger that I had not noticed before. I wanted to cry out a warning, but it was too late. One of the goblins bit in to the scaly snake part. A second later, the poor creature was staggering back, a bloody froth gushing from its mouth. Things seemed to slow down in that instant as I watched the acidic lamia blood carving its way down the poor goblin's throat. When the front of its little throat split open, I snapped out of my trance and went back to trying to figure out how to regroup.

There was a yelp, and I saw one goblin disappear down the lamia's throat in one gulp. I knew one thing that I would have to do despite the unsavory nature. In a single bound, I landed beside the remains of the dead little girl. I think I heard somebody hurl as I shoved it into my mouth to facilitate the healing of my damaged hands.

It wasn't enough. The fizzing goblin would have to be next. My only hope was that eating the creature did not do more harm than good. I guess the acid had a short half-life once it was out of the lamia. I barely felt a thing as I gulped down the little morsel that had once been one of my brave little goblins.

The bugbears were taking a different approach. They had swords. Sadly, their weapons appeared unable to pierce the lamia's hide. In a flash, that stinger whipped around and plunged into one of the bugbears. The howl of pain was brief. I wish the creature would have just died. What happened next was…unpleasant.

Spinning on his (or her) companions, I saw the eyes of the bugbear as they changed. They glossed over in a sickly green just before he swung his sword and decapitated one of his brethren. That was my cue. In a bit of a flying dropkick, I drove my switch toes into its chest. Two swipes later and I was stuffing bugbear bits into my gaping Sharkmouth.

Lisa staggered out of the trees and looked more than a little disoriented. I saw her draw her curved sword, holding it out in front of her, but a kitten could have swiped it aside. The lamia laughed with evil glee as she noticed the staggered Templar.

"Prepare for a nasty sting, warrior girl!" the lamia hissed.

"Is that the best you can do?" I scoffed as I charged, slamming into my target just before the tail arrived to deliver its terrible sting. "Aren't evil villains supposed to have witty lines for moments like this?"

The lamia simply hissed and showed her fangs. I climbed

off of Lisa and crouched to spring. Three more goblins lay sprawled on the ground, each nursing horrendous injuries from where they had scratched or clawed at the flesh of the lamia and been rewarded with a splash of blood that did far more damage to them than to her. Did they not see what was happening to their comrades?

I charged in and skidded to a halt as the tail to the lamia struck one of the goblins. The problem I'd had with being around those little mongrels for so long was that I could actually recognize one from the other.

"Butt Pimple!" I shouted. Any other time, that might have been funny. However, the agony in my voice made it clear that this was no laughing matter.

I could do nothing. The female goblin halted in her attack on one of the coils of the serpent woman and turned to face the closest goblin.

"Nose Wart, look out!" I screamed.

The goblin's reflexes were actually quite impressive. In a Matrix-style move, he bent himself back in a way that should have snapped his spine just in time to miss the blade that swished through the air. Just as fast, he came up and brought his own sword up and under the chin of the crazed female goblin. I guess I had expected him to hesitate; she was his mate after all. But no, he skewered her through the head and then kicked the body away as if it meant nothing.

I was wrong.

In a snarl of rage that would have sounded more normal coming from one of the bugbears, he flew at the tail of the lamia with his blade flashing. Up until this moment, the weapons had seemed to be ineffective against the scales of the lamia. But now I could see slices appearing as the blade struck home. Nose Wart gave one more agonizing scream and swung like a major league home run hitter. There was a spray of that caustic blood, but the stinger sailed through the air. There was something about what I was seeing, but I could not put my finger on it. The other goblins were all engaged in the assault, but I was seeing no evidence that they were managing to score any real damage.

Lisa had regained her feet. She shot me a look that might have been fear or anger. I was not exactly sure which one, but just that quick, she charged back into the fray.

I had no choice but to follow. The Templar came in low with a whirling dervish of a spin using the big blade that had been strapped to her back. I knew before it even connected that this was going to hurt. I was ready for the head of the lamia to go sailing. What I was not ready for was for the blade to almost stop with an audible clang as it struck the neck and bounced off as if the throat was made of high grade US steel.

"Foolish child!" the lamia hissed. "Your weapons are useless!"

Fangs dropped down and then she struck, her fangs plunging into Lisa's shoulder. Lisa was out of position to defend. I froze for a second as my friend screamed in agony. Tracers laced through her, and I could see the web-work of veins on any of her exposed flesh as a result of whatever poison was being pumped into her. Coils whipped around my friend in a flash that I think I was only able to actually see in detail because of my super ghoul senses.

Now it was my turn to scream in rage. The world seemed to fade with the exception of Lisa and that snake of a woman. I heard Aoife start to sing, but even the magic of her voice quickly faded as I rushed in with my claws. I did not care if the acid devoured me until I was nothing more than a puddle. I was not going to let this thing do whatever it had in mind to the one person that I loved more than I had ever loved anyone in my life.

I could smell something tasty, but I shoved that side as I cut and slashed. Something pulled on me. I think it was a bugbear. The poor thing was probably doing everything in its power to save me. Unfortunately, I think it got its belly opened in thanks as I swung and thrashed to get away and resume my assault on the hellish creature that had poisoned my Lisa.

I felt my hands sink into flesh. Unfortunately, I no longer knew who or what I was attacking. Rage filled me and threatened to burst me at the seams. I raged and swung, kicked, and at some point, I bit. Something foul filled my mouth and I felt pain course through me as acidic blood poured down my throat.

The vial!

The voice was faint; at the very outer most edges of my consciousness. I recognized the voice, but my wrath was in full swing, and it would not occur to me (until later) that it was Blodwen and Cody screaming in unison.

I *felt* the tiny glass bottle in a hand that was little more than a smoldering mess of fused bone; which is odd since I don't know how I would feel it if I no longer had any nerves left seeing as how the appendage had been melted away to almost nothing by this point.

"Eat this, bitch!" I think I growled. Considering the fact that my mouth was in almost the same condition as my hands and feet, I doubt anybody or anything nearby would have been able to decipher my words.

Still, somehow, I think I shoved that vial down the lamia's throat. All I can remember about that instant was a wave of cold that seemed to come from everywhere and coalesce on the vial as I crushed it against what I am pretty sure was the spinal column that ran down the length of the back of the throat of the lamia.

After that, there was nothing. Well, by nothing, I mean my mind went into DVR mode where the seven episodes of *American Horror Story: Freak Show* began to play on a loop. That poor two-headed girl.

That Ghoul Ava…On the Lam!

11

Mental Hopscotch

Something cold and delicious pressed against my lips. My mouth opened like that animatronic hippo from the Disney Jungle Cruise ride. Heck, maybe I even wiggled my ears.

"Keep your hands away from her when she is like that!"

I would be able to recognize that voice anywhere: Morgan. I forced myself to slip back into my little realm of mental reruns. Somewhere along the line, *American Horror Story* had been replaced.

"This is a story of two sisters, Jessica Tate, and Mary Campbell…"

Who knew that Rod Roddy would eventually become the "Come on down!" guy for Bob Barker on *The Price is Right*? Of course, *Soap* launched a lot of people into television stardom. I still think that it is perhaps the hands down, beat all and most hilarious television show in the history of the sitcom. Billy Crystal as a suicidal homosexual? And don't even get me started on the stuff that used to come out of Benson's mouth. Every single time that he said, "You want me to get that?" Absolute gold.

I never did understand what Tipper Gore had against that show. It ended way before its time. Of course, these days, people would be picketing and protesting the networks for some of the stuff that show pulled off.

Can I go off on a rant for just a second? Of course I can. I am I the grips of *Fame Rabia*. My body has undoubtedly taken catastrophic damage that I am trying to recover from. Most likely, Morgan is having me force fed every dead body she can get her hands on. But at least I managed to shove that vial down the lamia's throat—

Pain laced throughout my body. It came from my hands, my feet, my mouth, my throat. Hell, it would be easier to tell you where it did not come from. Back to Ava Land.

As I was saying, when Whoopi Goldberg needs to come on the screen to introduce my Bugs Bunny cartoons with an apology, we have gotten far too sensitive. Yeah, maybe there were some over-the-top caricatures of racial stereotypes, but in defense of Bugs and Daffy, we had just come out of a terrible war. The Japanese and German people were not exactly our pals. This country needed to laugh at our enemies or we would have undoubtedly all cried and slit our collective wrists.

I am not saying that we were not screwed up in a lot of ways. But they are behind us. Well, they are behind *some* of us. But can we pick the real fights and leave the petty things alone so that the important ones get the traction they deserve? We have become the culture that cried wolf.

"Ava?" a voice called form down a long, dark hallway. I knew the voice. From where I could not be sure, but it was very familiar.

"Mom?" I have no idea why I said that. The last person I would expect or even want to see at this point in my life would be that woman.

"She is obviously still delirious," the familiar voice tried to whisper, but to my hearing, she might as well have been shouting.

"Do we feed her again?" another familiar voice asked. This voice made me want to venture down the long dark hallway towards the light.

I felt myself floating in that direction, but the closer I got to that little rectangle, the more the pain cranked up. If this was some sort of dream state, should I feel myself breaking out in a cold sweat as I bit back the desire to scream? I didn't think so.

"Is she getting any better?" This voice belonged to a man! Again, I was struggling with the fact that the voice was familiar, but I could not have given a name to it if you held my hands over and open flame. Or dipped them in a vat of acid? Now why would I think of something like that? Who would dip another person's hands in acid? Even worse, why would somebody do that to *themselves*…willingly?

I retreated back to the darkness. Oh goody! *What's Opera Doc* is playing on the big screen in my mind! This was more like it. And besides, it wasn't like I could remember who any of those people…

Hmm, that's strange. What people? Why am I thinking about people? And why would I be doing something like that instead of watching Elmer.

"Kill da wabbit! Kill da wabbit!"

See? That is much more fun than trying to remember why I was trying to remember people that I can't remember.

More of my animated friends came to visit. There was Yak-ko, Wakko, and Dot, Pinky and the Brain, lots of Daffy, and even some Cartman thrown in for a bit of foul-minded humor. That poor Butters, he can't ever catch a break.

And that is how I passed my time. At least until that stupid fluffy bunny hopped up and sat down in front of me. And who was running the spotlight for that little rabbit?

"You need to start concentrating, Ava," the bunny insisted.

"Why do you sound like an old lady?" I asked the bunny.

"Fine, is this better?" and her voice was now that of a younger woman.

I could even tell that she was probably quite a looker. Why did I know that? I shoved all that away and leaned forward to give this bunny a closer look. It twitched its nose and scrubbed at its face with its little bunny paws.

"How did you get here?" I asked the bunny.

"I live here, Ava," the bunny sat up and gave a vigorous scratching behind one ear.

"You live in this dark place?"

I looked around. Nothing had changed. The room or whatever this place might be was still bathed in pitch black. In fact, this was strange. I can see in the dark.

Wait.

How did I know that?

If I could see in the dark, then, using that logic, I should be able to see right now. But the only thing that I could see was the fluffy little bunny in the spotlight. Well, that and the teensy, tinesy little rectangle of light that looked a million miles away at the moment.

"That is part of the problem!" The bunny was hopping up and down in front of me now. "Since you arrived, this place has been completely shrouded."

"And you want me to leave?"

"Yes!" another voice shouted. The cutest little lamb pranced out. Like the bunny, somebody was providing this little fella with its own spotlight.

"Aren't you just the sweetest little thing!" I was suddenly kneeling in front of the lamb, my arms around its neck.

"You're choking me!" the lamb coughed

"Oh, sorry." And just as quick, I was back sitting where I had been a minute ago. At least I think so. It was hard to tell with it being so dark.

"You need to go now, Ava. You are all better. It is time for you to return. They are counting on you," the lamb said rather insistently.

"They?" I asked.

"Shut up!" the bunny snapped, spinning on the poor defenseless lamb. "She has to do this on her own!"

I was about to ask what the lamb was talking about when I heard a low growl from somewhere deep in the darkness. It sounded far away; not as far away as the rectangle of light, but still a good distance.

"What's that?" I asked the bunny.

"Nothing to worry about. It is locked away safe and sound."

"But you said if she stayed much longer—" the lamb started, however, the bunny cut the cute little fella off.

"You have people waiting for you, Ava. They are counting on you." The bunny seemed to scratch its temple in thought. "They *need* you."

I heard the emphasis in that one word: *Need*. Something in my head told me that that was not a thing I should dismiss.

"But it is scary," I admitted. "And it hurts."

"The pain is temporary, Ava," the bunny assured me. "And as soon as you walk through that light, you will absolutely feel it tenfold. But they are ready for you and have what you need. It will only last for a little while."

The bunny was doing a terrible time of selling her idea. It would be like if McDonald's showed you the "after" picture of what a lifetime of eating their food would do to you—or just thirty days if you saw that Morgan Spurlock documentary.

"I'm scared."

The words were so puny sounding coming out of my mouth, but there was a sea of emotion in them. I had not fully realized it until that very moment, but it was the absolute truth. I was scared.

"No, that is impossible," the bunny corrected.

"What is impossible?" I asked.

"For you to be scared."

It was said with absolute sincerity. Well, I had news for this bunny, I was very scared. Scared of what was out there, scared of the pain I would have to face. And there was something else, but I could not quite nail it down.

"Ava, listen to me," the bunny hopped up onto the couch that I had not realized I was sitting on until this very moment, "there is a lot more to this than I am able to say."

"I don't get it." Something told me that was not the first time I'd said that in my life. And that was weird, because I just realized that I could not recall anything about myself. I kept getting flashes, but they may as well have been about somebody else, because if these were snippets of my life, they meant nothing.

"I wish I could tell you more, but it is prohibited. I fear the consequences of what might happen if I break those rules."

This was one very serious bunny. And where did that lamb run off to?

"But you are certain that I have to go? That I have to step through that rectangle of light at the end of that long hallway?"

"Umm…okay." The bunny looked around, its little floppy eared head scanning right past that doorway or whatever it was that I knew had to be the exit. But if she saw anything, she sure did not act like it.

"So I take it you don't see the door?"

"Sorry," the bunny said with an actual shrug of its tiny shoulders. The gesture was so damned cute that I wanted to scoop the little fur ball up and hug it. Or did I want to eat it?

Whoa! Where did that come from? I wondered.

"I will do this, but I sure don't want to," I finally agreed after a silence that seemed eternal, or just a few seconds. I could not tell.

That was just another odd thing about this whole situation. Time felt…funny…funny. Yep. That was the best way to put it. And no, not funny ha-ha; funny strange. For some reason, my mind was screaming something about Pink Floyd's *The Wall*. The problem with that was the fact that I had no idea what that was supposed to mean.

"Be strong, Ava!" the bunny called from far away.

That was funny, I did not recall having taken a single step. I was standing in the pitch darkness just on this side of the rectangle of light. I could hear hushed voices. They all sounded familiar. After a deep breath, I took that last step.

Then I screamed.

12

Owner of a Lonely Heart

"Ava! Ava, open your eyes!" a voice demanded.

I could feel hands on me. They were warm and soft and definitely belonging to a woman. Not that a man can't have soft, warm hands, but the fingers on these were dainty and delicate.

"I can't," I insisted. I had tried to open them a few seconds ago and the light had pierced my eye sockets and punched holes in my brain. Well, maybe not, but that is sure as hell what it felt like.

"Yes, you can. We have switched off all lights, you will be fine." There was a pause, and then almost as an afterthought, "Trust me."

"I don't see what the big deal is about her opening her eyes," Lisa grumbled. "She is here, so what's the big whoop?"

"The big 'whoop' as you so eloquently put it, is that she has not fully crossed over yet. A part of her mind is still within," Morgan lectured. From the sounds of it, I think they had gone over this a few times before.

"Hey, guys," I said in the softest whisper that I could manage, "I am right here. If you two need to keep yelling at each other, could you take it someplace else?"

"Oh, Ava," Lisa's voice sounded genuinely upset, "I am so sorry."

"There is nothing more to argue about." And then there was Morgan; stoic as ever.

I opened my eyes. Then, I screamed again.

***

I have no idea how much time passed. I do know that I heard and felt things around me. For instance, a tiny little clawed hand kept gripping mine. I began to notice a pattern. Usually within a few moments after I'd fed and then whoever had fed me left the room, there would be the slightest scrabbling of feet, and then the tentative grasp of that claw wrapping around my index and 'F-You' fingers.

It took me a while, but eventually, I figured out who it was. Funny, but I was so overwhelmed with relief that I couldn't speak that first time. I wish that I'd paid heed to that initial degree of emotional overload. Talking turned out to really suck.

"Hiya, Nose Wart," I said after feeling that last glorious lump of corpse slide down my throat, sending its healing powers throughout my body.

"Greeting, Just Ava," the goblin said after he made his way back from where he'd scrambled away, presumably due to my having just scared the bejeezus out of him—or, judging by the smell, perhaps something a little more bodily. In any case, he eventually re-took his seat at my side and took my fingers in his paw.

Then I stuck my stupid foot in my mouth. "How's Butt Pimple? She gonna be squeezing out little goblins any time soon?"

The wail that came from that little guy was heartbreaking. It sort of reminded me of Snoopy's howl from the cartoon...only way sadder.

Bits and pieces of the battle came to me. I was seeing things, but they were all disjoined and out of place. At least for a few seconds. Then it all fell magically into order.

Butt Pimple was dead.

"Oh, Nose Wart," I sighed.

I sat up and paid the price as my head began to spin and my stomach felt like it was about to turn inside out. I reached down and scooped the little guy up into my arms. He was stiff at first, and I think he might have actually believed in that instant that I was going to eat him.

My mind found that moment in time and replayed it. I saw the female goblin charge in. I also saw how quickly Nose Wart had dispatched her. I remember thinking that he'd done that without even a second thought.

"Had I a moment to go back, I would have let her kill me," the goblin whispered.

I was stunned. And then, I was ashamed. For some reason, I thought that goblins felt nothing like compassion or love. How could I have been so stupid? My mind brought up my first encounter with the jötunn. There had been real sorrow in the brother when I had hamstrung his sister. There was so much that I just did not understand about this new world. The Supernaturals liked to tell me all the time how I thought like a human and missed so much; but I think we are more similar to the mortal humans than they want to admit. The proof was in my lap, sobbing like a child…or a man who had just lost the woman he loved to a horrible tragedy.

"Your death would not have served a purpose. And then I would have probably ended up killing her," I said. As soon as the words came out of my mouth, I wanted to pull them back.

"My life serves no purpose now that my mate has died. I did not even get to honor her by consuming her."

I totally forgot! Goblins eat their mates when they die. I don't really know why; but I do know that a "taste test" is part of their courting ritual. Then another image came.

"You pulled me free of the lamia," I whispered. "You fed your beloved to me."

"You were in agony, Just Ava. My duty is to protect you to the death and with everything available to me," Nose Wart replied matter-of-factly.

I was stunned by the realization of what the goblin had done. But then the next part of that vision hit me like a truck.

The lamia had escaped. She had been hurt, of that there was no doubt, but she had not been killed.

"Who else did I lose?" I asked the goblin as I stroked the top of his head.

"We were able to save one of the bugbears and only nine of the goblins. Most perished from the damage they received when they bit into the lamia and swallowed her blood." Nose Wart sat up straight and looked me in the eyes. "Lisa was hurt pulling you up and out of the woods. But the witch died and Aoife was hurt terribly. She may not recover."

That made me stand. In fact, I stood so fast that I dumped poor Nose Wart to the floor. Of course, a second later I joined him as my head swam and I lost my balance.

The rest of the scene played out. It was a memory, but the best that I can do to relate it is to say that it was as if I was watching it through somebody else's eyes.

I saw me with my hands shoved down the lamia's throat. I was screaming with the pain. Rosanna rushed up chanting the words to activate the spell. The lamia's tail came around and slammed into her, but she climbed to her feet. Blood trickled from her mouth, ears, and nose. Yet, despite the obvious injuries that she had suffered, she resumed her chant. The second strike sent her flying into the brush.

Meanwhile, this entire time, I was screaming and cursing the lamia; she had her mouth clamped down on my arms and was shaking me like a puppy with a sock. When Rosanna crawled forward and resumed her chant; the lamia spat me out and spun on the witch. Lisa yelled something and the bugbears charged.

I had not yet had the time to try and figure out where my vision was coming from until I saw myself stand a few feet away. To say that I was in bad shape might be the understatement of the year. My arms were nothing but raw, ugly bone all the way to my elbows. It was with curiosity that I watched as I staggered a few steps and then sank to my knees. That was when Nose Wart rushed into view, only, he seemed to come from behind me; I would figure out why a second later.

The goblin gave me an appraising look and then turned to face where my vision came from. He looked right at me, but it was not me. It was—

Yes, Ava, you have consumed me and now I reside within you, the voice of Butt Pimple echoed in my head. I think I heard Blodwen chuckle.

I watched as Nose Wart leaned down to "me" and felt his soft kiss. I think he took a tiny nibble of my (and by that, I mean Butt Pimple's) cheek. Then, he scooped me up and carried me to the real me that was sprawled in the muck. A second or two later, it was dark.

Are you serious? I asked inwardly. *I thought that I only kept powerful Supernatural beings…no disrespect.*

She was the new queen of the clan having become the chosen mate for Nose Wart, Blodwen explained. "Umm…Nose Wart?" I said out loud. "I have some…good news?"

Actually, I didn't know if this was good or bad.

The goblin had his head cocked to one side and once again I was struck by how a goblin is very much like a dog in many ways. He crawled up my body in order to look me in my eyes. I blinked and he scrambled back and to a corner.

"How is that possible?" the goblin gasped. Actually, that statement shocked me. It was so overly coherent and…human. The problem that I had was that I did not know what he meant. Oh, sure, I had a hunch, but that couldn't be possible.

It is very possible, Blodwen corrected.

"She lives in your eyes?" Nose Wart whispered. It was almost a question and almost a statement. I could tell that he was confused, which made two of us.

They were very much in love, Blodwen explained.

Actually, that did not explain a thing. Not for me it didn't. Chalk it up to the steep learning curve, but this one had me perplexed. Did he see her in my eyes as if looking through a window, or did my eyes become hers for him? I was so confused.

You have it right with the first one, Blodwen said. *He can see inside to where she exists.*

And I can see him, Butt Pimple added.

Okay, everybody just hush for a minute and let me get my head around this, I said with a sigh. *Nose Wart can see her, and she can see him. Can he see you or Cody?*

Ask him, Blodwen said, and I could tell that she didn't know, which made me feel a little better about all of this confusion.

"Nose Wart?"

"Yes, Just Ava," he said with a pensive tentativeness.

That's cute, Butt Pimple snickered. *And very sweet of you to just leave that stand as it is since he would be greatly shamed if he knew that he was saying your name incorrectly.*

I would get back to her later on her sudden apparent leap in intellect. For now, I just wanted to clear the first item off my mental checklist of questions.

"Can you see just your beloved, or can you see others?"

Nose Wart scratched his head, and I saw the confusion as he processed what I had just asked. He came forward with the same degree of caution that he had used when we first met. It was like he was afraid of me all over again. At last he crossed the room and I knelt down so that he could peer in my eyes.

"I only see her." He waved one paw and then smiled. I had to assume that she waved back. When he leaned up even closer, I was caught off guard as he licked my eyeball!

"Okay! Never do that again!"

He scurried away and I instantly felt bad. I had to take a deep breath and make sure that my voice came out calm and as sweet as I could make it.

Ava! Blodwen scolded. *Taste! Remember? That is how goblins make many of their choices.*

"Yeah, yeah," I muttered out loud. "Listen, Nose Wart, I know how confusing this must be. Trust me, I can't make any sense from it either. However, please don't ever lick my eyeball again."

"Is that you, Ava?" a voice called down. It took me a second to realize it was Lisa. She sounded odd.

When she made her way down the stairs, I realized why.

Her entire head was bandaged to the point of looking like a giant Q-Tip. I recalled her taking a nasty hit during the fight, but that had to have been a while ago. Only, this looked fresh. If I had indeed been down with the *Fame Rabia*, then she would have had some time to heal. Unless she—

"Please tell me you did not try to take that lamia on by yourself while I was down," I said with a hint of anger in my voice.

"She has a name," Lisa groaned as she sat down in a chair. "Sheila has been a lamia for over three decades."

I could tell by the way she made that statement that it was of some sort of importance. Since she was ignoring my passive scolding for her having obviously gone after the dangerous monster without me, I decided that I would let her fill me in.

"Most lamias are consumed by their grief and guilt within five years or so. The fact that this one has been around for so long led me to try and find out how and why she still exists." Lisa looked up the stairs and then leaned forward in a conspiratorial manner that looked so out of place on this girl that I thought I knew but was just discovering. "She was employed by the Psychic Council."

Boom goes the dynamite.

"And let me guess," I kept my voice low since Lisa was obviously making the effort to do so. "They are coming for Morgan."

"Somebody wants her out."

"The easy guess would be Claude."

Lisa shook her head. "He is having his own problems it would seem. I guess the creatures under his rule have staged a revolt led by—"

"Please say it is an owlbear named Theodore."

"How did you know?" Lisa's head twitched in all those bandages and I had to guess that she had just raised her eyebrows in surprise.

"We can discuss that later. One problem at a time." I waved my hand. "So why is the council coming after Morgan?"

"Do you really need to ask?"

"Me?" I was not faking. I was truly caught off guard. Maybe I shouldn't have been after some of the stuff that I'd learned from Blodwen and the Templars when it came to my supposed significance as a female ghoul.

"We can worry about the council later," Morgan's voice came down from above like a scolding angel. In her always calm manner, she came down the stairs to join me and Lisa. "One problem at a time. This lamia has to be dealt with or we all run the risk of being exposed to a society that will not take the news of our existence well."

"What exactly would lead anybody to think this is something inhuman from the Supernatural world?" I asked. It seemed like a pretty obvious question considering the degree of brutality that I used to witness on the evening news back when I tried to watch it.

"Because she is becoming careless in her attacks. A human witnessed the last abduction."

I let that sink in and tried to imagine what the human that had seen this lamia must have thought. I know that I was having enough trouble with some of the creatures that I was encountering; and I was one of them! Sure, I was not some sort of evil child-abducting creature that ate her victims. I strictly ate the dead. Granted, I had helped a few of my meals reach that point, but as a habit, I was not a murderer.

"Okay, let's hear it," I finally said, using a rolling gesture with my hands to encourage the tight-lipped Psychic to spill the beans.

"Actually, we have the man in custody now and are having that bit of memory erased," a man's voice said as boots clomped down my stairs.

I tried not to react outwardly as Race Mitchell, Templar and mega hunk, came down into my basement. Of course I could actually have two different reactions to suppress if my hormones were not on instant overdrive at his surprise appearance. The first should really be concern. After all, the Templars were after me. I was Supernatural Enemy Number One. Of course, they were wrong in their assessment of me, but these were not the kind of people to wait and let you explain yourself.

Hmm…that was not entirely true. Race and his late partner Gordon had been more than patient when we'd first met. It was only when I ate Blodwen that things got twisted. And now, if I was to believe Lisa (which I did), Race was trying to find a way to essentially clear my name.

Race was wearing a chain mesh shirt and heavy leather pants that I initially mistook for being overly Bedazzled. Instead, they were, in fact, covered with little metal studs that looked sharp and pointy. He had a set of gloves hanging from his belt that looked like a weapon all by themselves. They were made from some sort of spun metallic fiber with three inch spikes over each knuckle.

I stilled the warm feeling in my tummy and ensured that my throat was clear before I spoke so that I would not sound so en-thralled. "You are erasing a human mind? That seems kind of cruel."

"Only the part regarding the lamia," Race said. He looked at me and smiled.

Down girl, I warned myself. This would take the term "sleeping with the enemy" to an entirely new level. Still, he had impossibly white teeth and the cutest dimples when he flashed that grin.

"So you can pluck out specific memories from humans?" I shot a look at Lisa who was apparently ignoring me at the moment. I couldn't blame her. Race is yummy. "You Templars have some pretty cool skills that border on kind of sketchy considering the fact that you are supposedly helping protect the human race."

"Oh," he laughed and his smile grew even wider on that amazingly rugged face, "we can't do anything like that."

"But you said—" I began to argue.

"We have a vampire helping with that particular task."

"Oh."

I felt kind of silly now. I mean, the Templars know so much about ghouls and I know next to nothing about them and what they can do other than some ring that extends their life and the fact that they manufacture weapons to be used specifically against certain Supernaturals.

"And this person that saw the lamia," I changed the subject just a little, "how are they going to account for being gone for however long it took you to capture them and erase their memory?"

"There are people who disappear all the time." Race shrugged. "This person is one of the lucky ones."

"How so?" I challenged. Having a memory enema did not seem all that lucky to me.

"This one gets to be found and reunited with his family."

He had a point. Still, it did get me to wondering how many missing persons stories from the past were because of things going on in the Supernatural world. I could not dismiss the fact that enough humans had been to blame, but I certainly did not believe that this was a new phenomenon occurring simply because of me.

(I wonder how many of you will be watching the news from now on with this same question bouncing around in your head. You're welcome.)

"So can I assume that this lamia, Sheila did you say was her name?" I glanced over at Lisa who nodded in the affirmative. "Can I assume that her lair or whatever you call it is still in the same place since somebody obviously went in and got trounced without me?"

"Actually, she did not go alone," Race spoke up. "She had a full squad of Templars with her. In fact, she was simply the lead scout and was not supposed to be involved in the engagement. She was injured trying to save some of her fallen comrades."

"Damn," I muttered. "And how many were with her?"

"Ten," Race replied with a grim face that did not look like it could be the same one that had flashed that thousand mega-watt smile just moments before.

"And how many survived?" I had to ask.

"Including Lisa?" Race managed to look even grimmer. I nodded. "One."

"She let me live," Lisa chimed in. I turned my attention to

her and saw her eyes shining with tears that were welling up as she spoke. "She wanted me to return and give Morgan her ultimatum."

"She has an ultimatum," I snorted. "Of course she does. Personally, I think it is a bit too stereotypical of an evil villain, but I'm game, let's hear it."

"She is to turn you over," Lisa said with abrupt bluntness.

It took a few seconds for that to sink in. She meant me! How had this become all about me. (Chantal the ghost reminded me that the series is titled *That Ghoul Ava*, so I guess that is as good of a reason as any.)

"Turn me over to whom?" I asked, making sure to keep Race in my field of vision. He had seemed just a little bit jumpy when Lisa dropped the big reveal.

"To the Templar," Race said when it was clear that my friend was not going to answer.

"So the Psychic Council is working with the Templars to bring me in?" I asked. "And both groups are okay with all the children being killed in this little game of chess?"

"Actually…no."

I absolutely did not know the owner of that voice.

I was about tired of all the surprises. This was a big one since it was a man that I had never seen before. He was pretty average when it came to height—I guessed him at just around five foot ten. That was the last thing about him that was in any way able to be considered average.

He had short brownish hair and dark, chocolate brown eyes that made my knees buckle just a bit when they locked on to mine. He was Rob Lowe pretty. In fact, he looked almost identical to the *St. Elmo's Fire* version. He had that perfectly kissable mouth that I remember from my posters. Not that I kissed…oh, who am I fooling? Of course I kissed Rob Lowe in that poster.

As he came down into my basement, I noticed how everybody seemed to automatically step back and give him room. Even Race looked to automatically defer to this man. That made me assume that he was some Templar muckity-muck. You know what they say about assuming.

105

"Ava, please let me introduce Edward Losli, Supreme Psychic." Morgan extended her arm and dropped to one knee.

13

Voices Carry

"Excuse me?" I spat, so surprised that my fingers and toes went switch.

"Relax, Miss Birch." Edward brought his hands up in some sort of half-hearted gesture of placation that did nothing for my nerves.

One problem was the fact that I actually had no idea why I was so suddenly on edge. It wasn't like I'd heard terrible stories about this so-called Supreme Psychic. In fact, I had not known until this very moment that such a person (or thing) existed.

"Easy for you to say," I muttered.

"I assure you that I am not here to do you any harm," Edward said in his amazing voice that I just knew could belt out a tune if he was so inclined. "I want to start by disavowing whatever it is that the Psychic Council has set out to do."

"Is it true that Psychics can't lie?" I blurted before I had a chance to think of a better (or more tactful) way to ask this question.

"It is, Ava," Edward said with a slight nod of his head. "And before you ask, yes, our long lives have given us plenty of time to learn how to answer a question truthfully with information that is often misleading and that many would consider a lie. However, I want to assure you that I am most interested in working *with* you, not against you. I have plans for you and Morgan in the future and believe that we can become friends."

I glanced over at Morgan, but she was not giving up anything. I was a bit intrigued by how she was taking the whole idea of me being "friends" with her boss. If I knew her at all, I was willing to bet that she was grinding her teeth down to nubs— figuratively speaking of course since she was so adept at hiding anything that resembled emotion.

Personally, the thought of being friends with a Psychic did not seem likely. But if he was up for a bit of blanket bouncing, we could absolutely talk.

My word, you have been without for quite some time, haven't you, dear? Blodwen piped in.

Something I never understood about humanoid beings, Butt Pimple added. *If the desire to rut arises, then why not simply fulfill it? Especially if you are female. I have yet to meet a male that will not have his trousers around his knees at even the slightest hint that there is the opportunity for sex.*

Yes, agreed, Blodwen continued.

They make a good point, Cody spoke up.

I shut them out and returned my attention to what was going on around me. As I scanned all the faces, I realized that I was the center of attention. It was not a comfortable feeling.

"So who is behind wanting me turned over?" I asked.

"There are factions within the council that have taken a more radical view of things with your arrival on the scene. A female ghoul was not supposed to ever be seen again," Edward said with a careful deliberation that made me certain that he was selecting his words very carefully. "And a recent development has put this faction in league with a group of Templars who also seek your eradication."

"I still don't understand how anybody can support an idea that allows for innocent children to be murdered with such horrific brutality," I said.

"And it is for that very sentiment that I am certain that you have nothing in common with some of your more infamous female ancestors," Race spoke.

He stepped a little in front of Edward, and if I did not know better, I would have thought he was showing a hint of jealousy. Of course that could simply be my wishful thinking. I don't know of any woman who is being honest with herself that would not want a pair of very hot, mature men squabbling over them (mature, not old; although they both actually qualified in the literal sense as being ancient).

"All of this is wonderful, but perhaps she should know who is actually behind this." Morgan elbowed both men aside—literally.

"Yes, a name that I believe you are familiar with," Edward said with a nod; although I did see the nasty glance he shot Morgan. I don't think Psychic bosses like being elbowed aside by their employees or lower management types any more than their human counterparts. "Blumegastrickfiggernilly."

Yep, I knew the name. He was the regional Psychic for the Oregon Coastal part of the state. He had actually made me an offer once upon a time. I refused it obviously. There had been something about that guy that I did not care for when we met. Now I was seeing my decision as a rather smart one.

Nose Wart knew the name also. He made a little squeak and ducked behind me like that could keep anybody from taking notice of his existence.

That ruptured lesion on the anal sac of a mangy dog! May his testes grow to the size of melons and rupture.

Glad to see that Butt Pimple had retained her goblin ability of creative cursing. I felt Nose Wart peer around my leg and I had to wonder for a second if he was perhaps able to hear his beloved as well.

"Is he come to take us back?" the goblin asked, putting an end to my speculation.

"No, little goblin," Edward said in a way that did not make me think he was being dismissive to Nose Wart in the slightest. That scored points. "It is Ava that Blue wants, and it seems that he is willing to do anything to have her."

Again, I have to use the dog analogy, but for any pet owners, you all know the place those four-legged creatures keep in our hearts. For many of us, the dogs and cats of the world are far more valuable to us than most of our human acquaintances. We mourn their loss with even more tears in many cases. Nothing set my radar off quicker than the visible disapproval of one of my pets towards a new person in my life. Furthermore, I was also very cognizant of how others treated their furry companions. Anybody who could abuse or neglect an animal deserved far greater punishment than our current legal systems mete out.

I often believed that a suitable punishment should match the crime. Can you imagine if we could send all those people who fought their Pit Bulls to some sort of caged arena where they had to fight bare-handed to the death with others of their ilk? Or maybe shove those puppy mill types into a small plastic crate and just leave them there to stew in their own filth with little to no food or water? Hmm…good thing I will never be president…or Queen of America.

"So let him have me," I said after a long pause. Before they could all kick in their assorted protests, I laid out my reasoning. "Get him to promise to recall this lamia in exchange for me. Make sure that she is brought back first before handing me over. I am assuming that you Templars have a weapon designed to kill the bitch or you wouldn't have gone after her."

"Actually," Race spoke up with what sure looked like embarrassment, "we thought we did. Only, there is a rumor that this particular lamia has made some sort of pact with a demon. Our only known weapon is useless. That is also why your witch failed."

It hit me like a landslide. I had all but forgotten about Rosanna. Oh, my God! And Aoife, too! Apparently I staggered, because Race and Edward both lunged for me as I toppled back onto my butt with a graceless thump.

"Where is Aoife?" I demanded once I got past the shock.

"She is being tended to by others of her kind that are more skilled at treating the types of injuries that she suffered.

"And what of Rosanna?" I realized that I did not actually recall her going down. I'd only been told that she was dead.

"There was not enough left of her to even bring home,"

Morgan said coolly.

"Do you know any other witches that can whip up that potion?" I asked.

"Yes, but the invocation would not be possible. No witch will touch this now that word of Rosanna's demise and the cause has reached their ears." Morgan gave a dismissive wave of her hand.

"Actually, I think you guys have made it a point to stay too out of touch with the times. Could she make the invocation via phone?" I looked around the room and saw blank expressions at first, but slowly, the light began to dawn on each of them as they gave my idea some consideration.

"Let me get in touch with another of my witches." With that, Morgan hurried up the stairs.

"I seem to have underestimated you, Ava," Edward said with a sweeping gesture that ended in a bow. "Perhaps I gave too much credence to the reports that came in from others."

I kept my mouth shut. I did not need to be hit in the head with a hammer to know that Morgan would be primary among those so-called *others* to whom he was referring.

"Yes, well, I never underestimated you for a moment," Race quipped. Again I was sort of enjoying this little game of one-upsmanship taking place between these two very different men. I shot a look over at Lisa and saw her lips curving up in a smile. She was seeing it too! Yay, I wasn't being delusional!

Don't kid yourself, dear, Blodwen snickered, being fully aware of my thoughts. *You can be quite delusional when you put your mind to it*.

"You can't be serious about giving yourself over like this."

I started. Somehow, even in her obviously wounded state, Lisa had made her way to my side. I looked over and was hit by it instantly. Since becoming a Templar, she had almost lost any of the human smell that equates to the closeness that they are to death. You all have it; because, let's face it, you all die a little bit each day.

When Lisa had put on the Templar ring, it had all but halted her inevitable march to that last breath. And now that she was supposedly out of her novice phase, she had a more decorative ring. I'm not all that hip on the ins and outs of the whole Templar thing, but the fact remained that I should not be able to smell her. Yet, here I was getting a good whiff of my friend and she smelled delicious.

"How bad are you hurt?" I asked, brushing her comment aside.

Lisa seemed caught off guard by my question. She glanced over to where Race and Edward stood and then back to me.

"Not here…not now," she whispered. I don't know who she thought she was fooling; those two men were enhanced and could probably hear a fly walking on the other side of a concrete wall.

I decided to remedy the situation. I turned to the two men. "Out. Now."

To their credit, neither said so much as a single word. They both gave a nod and headed up the stairs. Now it was just me and Lisa—and Nose Wart, but for some reason, I was fine with him sitting right there at my feet.

"How bad," I insisted.

Lisa's shoulders sagged slightly and her hands came up to the bandages that wrapped her head. She very gently began to peel them away. I watched, but a small voice inside me (not belonging to any of my mental residents) told me that I did not want to see what she was about to show me.

It was worse than I imagined. She had a horrible burn that had stripped most of the left side of her face down to the bone. In fact, I had no idea how she was even alive. The fact that she had not lost her left eye was a miracle. It looked like it could fall out if she so much as sneezed. I could see her teeth as her cheek was basically gone, and they were ugly and blackish.

There was also a nasty puncture on her left shoulder and I recalled how she had taken that injury in that fateful encounter that had gone so bad so fast. It looked horribly infected and I had to once again wonder how she was even managing to stand, much less function.

I looked at her and nodded for her to please explain. I would have used my words, but I did not trust my voice at this point. One thing a ghoul knows is death and dying. Lisa was dying.

"The poison she pumped into me during that first attack won't clear out," Lisa finally said, her eyes not meeting mine for some reason. "A Templar is supposed to have the ability to flush their system of any toxins. It is really quite simple. If we are to constantly be putting ourselves through such dangerous conditions, one of the magicks in the ring is like the ultimate antioxidant. And what is even cooler is that you can feel it cleaning your system."

I glanced at her hand and saw the ring in question. It was glowing a dull golden hue, but it was glowing. I had to assume that meant that it was working. So why wasn't she getting better?

"Did you know that I was genetically predisposed to contract breast cancer?" Lisa smiled weakly. "My boobs tingled for three days. It was really weird. I sort of wish I could pass this ring around at a hospital. Wouldn't it be great if we could wipe out disease so easily?"

"You are trying to avoid the topic," I said with a gentle nudge to her side.

"Yeah, I guess I sort of got attached to the idea that I was gonna live forever."

"Nothing lives forever," I said with a shake of my head. "Look at how many supposed immortal beings I have taken down. Sure, we aren't talking Jack Bauer numbers, but I have killed a few bad guys that thought they would live forever. A few were older than Morgan."

I'm not technically dead, Blodwen grumped.

How do you know I meant you? I shot back. *Now hush, this is important.*

Yeah, you slapping her with mortality as she knocks at Death's door is probably really being helpful.

"I should be okay by now." Lisa sat down on the gurney that I'd been occupying while I recovered. "But I am having to fight this poison with all my being. I think that is weakening me to the point where it is countering the lethal effects of the lamia's toxin."

"What do you mean you are fighting the poison?"

"Right now I am warring with the desire to kill you and everybody here."

Nose Wart made a little growl and I scooted him back before he could take another step closer to Lisa. Hearing that little revelation made me just a bit nervous. How would I react if she suddenly turned on me? I mean, if she went after Morgan, that would be one thing, but me?

"I have an idea," I said suddenly.

Lisa gave me a look that showed her lack of confidence in my ability to come up with something that she had not yet tried. I would be hurt later, but right now, I was going to do anything in my power to help my friend.

"Lie down." I pointed to the gurney she was currently sitting on.

"I don't think we have time for—" Lisa began, but I cut her off.

"Just do it and stop being a Templar for a minute. You are not going to be joining me on this little adventure anyway. I have an idea. It might seem stupid, but at this point isn't it worth trying everything"

Lisa gave me a dirty look, probably because of the 'stop being a Templar' comment, but at least she finally laid down on the gurney like I asked. I looked around and spotted what I needed hanging on the wall. Hmm, somebody had gone through a lot of trouble to organize everything down here. There was a peg board with the tools all outlined and everything.

"Nose Wart, go get me that set of chains hanging on the wall." I turned back to Lisa and smiled. "Now I just need you to trust me for about five minutes. After that, if this does not work, well, at least I tried. But even then, I will probably try something else because I will not just sit here and let you die this slow and apparently agonizing death."

"Here you go," Nose Wart said, handing me the chains and scampering away to a far corner.

"Umm, Nose Wart, is there a problem?" I asked this just as I noticed the slight burning sensation in my hands. I looked down to see the skin smoldering. Out of reflex, I dropped the chains.

"Ava?" Lisa sat up, concern etched on her face. "Are you okay?"

"That hurt." I shook my hands and turned to Nose Wart who now looked like he was about to wet himself. I liked him better when he was a fearless warrior. I was not a fan of the wimpy goblin thing he had going on.

He thinks you are going to eat him, Butt Pimple spoke up.

Why would I do that?

He just handed you silver chains and you can see how you reacted to them.

"But I asked him to do it." I might have yelled that last remark outwardly as loud as I had inwardly.

I was struck for an instant about how I had not known until this minute that silver did anything to me. Wasn't that for werewolves and vampires?

"Are you okay?" Lisa asked with genuine concern.

"Nothing a little snack can't take care of," I answered. It was then that I realized all the residual pain that I'd felt when I first opened my eyes had faded to the background. Basically it had become the equivalent to a nasty headache. It sucked, but it was not migraine-style debilitating.

Of course the "little snack" comment made Nose Wart flinch. I would have to sit him down later and have a talk. I would no sooner eat him as I would a new puppy.

Bracing myself for the pain, I grabbed the chains and motioned for Lisa to lie back down. As soon as she did, I went to work wrapping her up. A few minutes and a handful of padlocks later, and Lisa was secured to the table.

I stepped back and called over my shoulder for Nose Wart to bring me a body from the freezer chest. It thudded to the ground beside me and I made short work of it. Once my hands were healed and my other pain was now just a distant ache that I could completely block out with almost no effort, I looked down at Lisa.

"Let your hate flow through you," I said in a terrible impersonation of Emperor Palpatine.

I loved that scene in the last real *Star Wars* movie. It was the tipping point for the redemption of somebody that you had spent years believing to be the ultimate evil in the universe.

"What are you talking about?" Lisa asked, snapping me out of my little daydream where Han Solo and I kiss on Endor while the ewoks drag that silly princess away as she pitches a royal fit.

"You said that you are fighting the urge to go on some sort of Templar *jihad*. Well, give in to that feeling. Let that anger come."

"Oh dear!" Nose Wart gasped and scampered up the stairs leaving just Lisa and me in the basement.

That might be the smartest most ridiculous idea I've ever heard, Blodwen said with genuine appreciation.

"But—" Lisa protested. I put a finger over her mouth and shushed her.

"Just do it."

Lisa closed her eyes. I took a step back. I was not sure if Templars had super strength that might enable her to snap out of those chains. If so, I had a less desirable plan.

Be ready for a new roommate if this fails, I warned Blodwen, Cody, and Butt Pimple.

Lisa's eyes snapped open. Only, they weren't hers. They were a sickly green where the whites should be. Her mouth curved in a sneer of hatred that made me take another few steps back. I've had my share of dirty looks shot at me over the years. This was so different. It was the embodiment of hatred. It hurt my heart to see Lisa look at me that way. However, her ring began to glow brighter.

"What's the matter, little toy soldier? Is the nasty ghoul just out of your reach."

"Why don't you take a step closer and say that, you skanky little bitch!" Lisa snarled. "In fact, loosen these chains and let's see what you got. I won't even use a sword. I will tear you apart with my bare hands and stomp your skull until what little brains you possess squirt on the floor."

Ouch, I thought, *I sure hope that this was the poison talking*

116

and that it had not perhaps just loosened Lisa's tongue to the point where her actual feelings about me were being expressed.

"Ava!" I heard Morgan and Race both bark as they hurried down the stairs.

"What have you done?" Morgan gasped as she came to a halt beside me.

"Look who showed up. Just like you to arrive after the fact so that you don't have to take any responsibility. I am going to enjoy ending you. Maybe I will rip out your throat so that you can experience what that childhood friend of yours had to endure when the vamps got her."

Lisa was referring to a story that Morgan had shared about her childhood…which just happened to be around the time that the *actual* Jesus was alive. That was absolutely not the Lisa I knew. This person was just plain nasty.

"Let me guess, Ava," Lisa laughed with uncharacteristic cruelty, "Doing a little mental spacing out that you try to use as an excuse for the degree of cluelessness that you possess?"

"Wow," Race murmured as he came down the last few stairs and stood beside Morgan. "She has a real nasty streak."

"Race Mitchell, Templar and my trainer. Do you think that I have not noticed the way you stare at my tits? Perhaps it was okay for older men to take young brides in your time, but now that is known as being a pedophile."

I was reminded of *The Exorcist*. There was a scene when the girl was strapped down and talking to the priest. She said some pretty foul things. Right now, that girl was an angel compared to Lisa.

"Good news." Morgan turned away from where Lisa was turning a deep crimson as she struggled against the chains that held her bound to the gurney. "It would seem that one of my witches believes that your idea just might work. Of course that would be contingent on somebody not taking your phone."

"Does Race know that you want to fu—" I spun and punched Lisa in the face. Her head snapped back and her eyes rolled back in her head.

"Oww!" I bent over clutching my hand left hand with my

right.

There was a silence that stretched into uncomfortable. It was Nose Wart that actually came to the rescue. "If Just Ava is giving herself over to Psychic Blumegastrickfiggernilly, then I will be coming with her, as will the other goblins. We have a score to settle with some of our kin."

"This is not the time—" Morgan began, but I had another spectacular idea. It seemed like I was on a bit of a roll.

"They would make great cover. Hard for somebody to keep all the balls in the air when people keep lobbing shots at you," I blurted, cutting her off.

"Fine, then let's go." Race said with a nod.

We headed up the stairs, but I shot Lisa one last glance. My eyes came to rest on her ring. It was so bright that it hurt my brain. It might have only been wishful thinking on my part, but I could almost swear that she was looking better already.

14

Back for More

The Hummer came to a stop and Morgan looked over her shoulder to where I sat in the backseat. I'd been staring out the window, watching the scenery change from the mountains that we'd had to drive through to reach the coastal town of Tilla-mook. I'd started seeing the territorial markings of the Cow Fart clan of goblins under the control of Blumegastrickfiggernilly—or just plain Blue if we were being informal. Something told me this was not an informal meeting.

Nose Wart and his fellow members of the Castrated Mallard clan were all stuffed in the cargo area. They'd been remarkably silent during the ride. Not only that, but Butt Pimple's presence had basically vanished.

We set out just after sunset to maximize the time I would have. Of course, Morgan had sent somebody (or something) to ensure that the Sheila the child-murdering lamia was gone. Once it was confirmed, we made the final preparations.

The new witch had arrived that afternoon to deliver the vial. I hadn't liked her, and so I had not bothered to even learn her name. In fact, when I looked at her, I could actually see her en-joying that little ritual that made Aoife and all sirens hate witches.

She handed me a phone that only had one number on auto

dial: hers of course. And the entire time she was going over the directions—despite the fact that I had told her Rosanna had already prepped me—she talked to me like I was stupid. I could see her and Morgan being real pals.

I spent that entire day down in the basement. Lisa was no more pleasant when she woke, but since I was the only one down there, I just tuned her out and ignored the vile filth coming from her mouth.

"She will be okay," Morgan whispered, snapping me back to the here and now.

"I hope so." I scanned the parking lot, searching for Blumegastrickfiggernilly and his entourage.

"That was actually quite clever," Morgan said. That comment almost made me jump out of my skin.

"Did you just give me a compliment?" I gasped.

"Would you rather I not?"

The problem (or, should I say *one* of the problems) I have with Morgan is her lack of emotion when she speaks. You can never tell if she is being serious or joking. Considering how seldom she would probably joke around, it was always just easier to make the assumption that she was being serious. That was how I had taken that last comment. Then she smiled. It was so slight that I would have missed it if not staring at her face and having perfect vision in the dark. But it was a twitch of the corners of her mouth in the upwards direction. That was a smile; a tiny one, but a smile none the less.

"I have told you before, Ava. I see great value in you. I have always expressed it in the payments that you receive for the jobs that you complete. However, I am very happy that you have stayed in my district. I rely on you perhaps more than I have ever relied on another being."

For once in my life, I was actually speechless. While I would never think for a second that Morgan and I could bond, I had not realized until that exact moment just how much her approval and acceptance meant to me. A few witty retorts poked up, but I shoved them down, determined not to ruin this "moment."

"Thank you." That seemed simple and satisfactory.

"Now, be very careful. We can only hope that Blumegastrickfiggernilly is as blissfully unaware of technology as…" Morgan paused, the next words out of her mouth would be an admission of ignorance, "…as many others in the Supernatural community."

Nice way to duck the admission of her lack of knowledge when it came to everyday devices that humanity had used to shrink the world to the point where a sneeze in Tokyo meant a mutant strain of the flu would be crippling Dubai in a week. Sometimes it paid to still think like a human. That was not to say that I did not have a problem with the fact that none of them had thought of this before. Rosanna might very well still be alive if somebody—namely me—might have mentioned such an idea before. The reality was that that tiny witch was in no way equipped for what she had walked into. I would carry that guilt forever most likely.

I stepped out of the vehicle, barely aware that the goblins were all pouring out in my wake and dashing off into the darkness. I wondered briefly if I would ever see Nose Wart again.

I have no such doubts, Ava, a female goblin's voice whispered from the recesses of my mind.

I shoved her back into where she needed to be right now. I wanted no distractions. I needed to be fully aware of what was around me. This was going to go down fast if my guesses about this Psychic were correct. The Hummer pulled out of the parking lot and I waited until the lights vanished from view before I ventured forth.

When we'd met that first time, he had rubbed me the wrong way. I had a feeling that he no longer wanted me as his own personal enforcer. Why would he when he had a lamia?

The parking lot to the strip mall looked empty, but it did not feel that way at all. My skin practically crawled with the sensation of the eyes that were on me.

My only warning came in the snarl directly behind me. I ducked on instinct and shot my leg out and did a roundhouse kick to my left and back. I heard the yelp as my switch toes cut off a limb. I was not sure yet if it were arm or leg, and I didn't care.

The fight was on. I popped back up and was just a little up-set to discover that my opponent was hardly injured at all. I had not severed a limb, but instead managed to cut the telephone pole-sized club that he had been carrying. The creature standing before me was hideous. And not in that way that goblins are so ugly they are cute.

This behemoth was a wart and boil covered monstrosity. He was easily ten feet tall. His head sat firmly on his shoulder with no real sign of a neck and looked about a third of the size that it needed to be to match the rest of him. And yep, I knew it was a him because "him" was naked. And apparently fighting was some sort of turn on. His skin was ruddy and crisscrossed with scars. That meant he'd seen more than a few fights.

"What's the matter, Blumegastrickfiggernilly?" I shouted as I ducked under a wild swing with the half of a telephone pole this beast still had as a weapon. "You scared to fight a girl?"

It was a weak attempt, I will grant you that, but you can't blame a gal for trying. I spun and ducked as another swing came from this beast in an overhand smash that I imagine was de-signed to turn me into pulp. I had a small opening and took it as I brought my right hand up and drove it into the middle of one of the tautest beer bellies that I have ever seen in my life.

The creature barely seemed to notice. In the meantime, I scarcely had enough time to yank my hand back and throw my-self to the right as he brought his backhand around, clipping me on the side of my head. Seriously, he barely grazed me and bells were ringing. I managed to shake it off in time to avoid his stomp that would have turned me into Ava jelly.

I took a few steps back and the monster cocked its head to one side as if hearing something. When his mouth practically split his face in half because of the smile, I went to hyper-alert. Not that I wasn't paying attention before, but something bad was about to happen. It was as plain as the smashed nose on that tiny, ugly, wart-covered face of his.

My caution was rewarded…sort of anyway.

A second one of these creatures leapt from the roof of the strip mall and landed with a ground shaking thud. They could have been twins. Of course that was how I'd felt about goblins when I'd first encountered them; I imagine that these things probably had their own uniqueness. I simply wasn't seeing it.

If I was doing well just to keep this one at bay, I had my doubts as to how this fight was about to go now that there were two. Setting my feet, I was in a place to be able to have them in front of me for the most part. Of course, they were a lot smarter than they looked. They had moved out to my sides so that I sort of had to turn my head back and forth just a bit to keep them both in view.

I recalled my first battle with the jötunn children. That was the unfortunate part; they had been children and were obviously inexperienced in combat. These two knew what they were doing.

One would feint and come in just enough to get me to turn more in his direction; that would allow the other to lunge and swing. I paid for my missteps twice. One barely grazed my shoulder and merely staggered me. However, the second one caught me flush and sent me flying like a lazy curveball over the heart of the plate. I rolled two or three times and skidded to a halt on my back.

Getting to my feet, I noticed the snow starting to fall. My mind went into damage control mode. I was caught off guard when "Let it Snow, Let it Snow" started playing in my head. At least it was the cool version by Brian Setzer.

I made up my mind that I was going to have to take these guys down one at a time. Fighting them as a pair would end in failure. I wasn't too convinced that I was going to come out of this anyways. I might as well at least try to take one of Blumegastrickfiggernilly's minions down in the process.

The closest one was a good ten yards or so away and to my right. I feinted left and then leapt. This was going to either go well, or I was going to be splattered like an overripe melon. Luck was with me as I caught the monster off guard. He had bitten on my fake and took all ten switchtoes in the chest.

I didn't have much time to enjoy this small victory. I flipped back to free myself and caught his backhand as my reward. It was a surprise, because I had overestimated the damage that I had inflicted. However, his companion had also misjudged my ability to recover. By the time he was standing over me with his club about to come down on my head, I drove up with two hands. This strike proved fatal. I actually felt the massive pump that served as his heart. One flick and I filleted it and ended his day on the spot.

Unfortunately, that had allowed the other, despite the toe gouges I'd inflicted leaking a grayish blood from ten punctures in its chest, to come in and punt me the distance of this parking lot. I wish I would have landed in the tall grass, but instead, I came to a wet splat in the mud of the nearby lake.

By the time I pulled myself free, he was on me again. This time he connected with an overhead smash that drove me to my knees. Thankfully he had tossed his busted club aside and had been content to use his massive fist. I felt my left shoulder separate. In fact, I had to look twice to ensure that my arm was still attached.

I fell back on something I saw in a movie once. Heck, I don't even remember which one. But I started to stagger, almost falling to my knees. As I'd hoped, the beast came in for the blow that he believed would take me out for good. Just as he did, I rolled forward, and with a backhand swipe, I hamstrung him in both legs. He toppled, and I dove into his back with my one good hand. I don't care what you are, five of my switchfingers in the back of your skull will take you out of commission.

The lake was churning and I already had a good idea what was coming. I cut away a few slabs of this dead thing and stuffed them into my mouth. I could feel the shoulder knitting already. I had time for one more bite, and I don't know that it even touched the sides of my mouth with me having stuffed it down so quick.

I got to my feet as the lake troll rose from the murky waters. Last time I'd seen it, the creature was snacking on faerie. I was not about to be part of its diet. I started to back up a few steps. I think I was secretly hoping that it would not be able to leave the water.

I was wrong.

The best news I got was when this thing came out of the lake. I guess that little pond has a flat bottom (most likely for the summer tourists who pay way too much to rent the paddle boats). The lake troll was only about forty feet tall. Notice how I say "only"? A ghoul has to find a win where she can.

"You defeated my ogres, bitch, but let's see how you fare against the lake troll," a voice called from somewhere. He actually sounded kind of tinny like an old recording or that creepy voice from the song "Winchester Cathedral."

Hey, at least I knew what I'd just fought. However, I was actually more concerned about this lake troll than I had been a pair of battle-hardened ogres. This thing could swallow me whole. Its mouth looked big enough to fit a bouncy house inside.

I let it come to me, but I was also scanning the area for any other nasty surprises. I was not expecting this to play out like some Bruce Lee movie. By that, I am talking about how Bruce would always end up cornered by twenty or thirty evil henchmen. Only, instead of them just pulling a dogpile-on-the-rabbit move and bum rushing little Brucey, they come in ones and two so that he can beat the holy dog snot out of them all. I never did understand that. Maybe Blumegastrickfiggernilly was dumb enough to only send one of his nasty minions at a time.

It only took the lake troll three steps to cross the length of probably half of a football field. *I guess one at a time might be enough*, I thought as I went blank on how I might take this thing on and have a chance. The creature came to a halt and eyed me. I was barely a snack to this thing.

I was going to have to fight this lake troll defensively. That was my brilliant plan. I would wait for it to attack so that I could see how it operated, then I would just counterattack based on that. Sort of like saying, I will let you punch me in the face and then hope I hurt your hand enough so that you didn't want to do that again.

For those of you who have forgotten from that first encounter, a lake troll is a rotten shade of brown and green. It is covered in what could be either moss or hair, and it has huge, saucer-shaped eyes that are a purplish color. It does not have a proper nose; more like two slits that open and close as it breathes. Oh…and then there are those five or six rows of jagged teeth that looked sort of like alligator teeth.

"What are you waiting for? Destroy her!" the invisible Psychic with the funny name bellowed from seemingly everywhere at once.

It was now clear to me that Blumegastrickfiggernilly was scared of me. That was the only explanation. Why else would he not have simply come out to greet me and maybe gloat over my having no choice but to sign on with him? I mean, sure I could have sent back a refusal, but then more children would have been killed; and that would have weighed heavily on my conscience. Only, at the moment, my plan was not looking so good.

The lake troll craned its neck around. "She has pokey bits, me no want pokey bits on my tongue," the lake troll protested in a deep, wet voice that was only sort of fitting.

Actually, the voice almost made me laugh. Maybe I should explain. This thing had almost a British accent; or maybe it was Scottish. Did lake trolls originate in the UK or something?

"Just destroy her!" came the reply from all around.

"What's the matter, Blue?" I shouted. "You scared of little old me? Why not just send out that little lamia skank and let me take her on. I got a score to settle with her."

I needed a better writer. I was simply too nervous about the giant lake troll at the moment and the fact that he wanted to gobble me up except for the fact that I had "pokey bits" that were causing him some concern to make some sort of clever retort.

"No, you will not be facing Sheila, my foolish little ghoul," Blumegastrickfiggernilly snarked. "She would kill you, and I want you alive."

I was not following his logic. I mean, those ogres were trying to pound me into road kill. Now I was facing something that wanted to eat me. In what world would he be getting me alive?

"If you want me alive, why not just come out and take me yourself?" I challenged. "It's sort of like being the guy who is trying to bust in the door only to have somebody walk up and turn the knob."

I want you out of commission for a little while," Blumegastrickfiggernilly replied. "But don't worry, I know how to handle the *Fame Rabia*. You would be right as rain in a few weeks, and by then I would be done with a handful of things that would ensure that you remained in my employ without incident."

I had no idea what nasty scheme he had in mind, and I did not want to find out. Still, I had to wonder how I would be okay after being eaten by the lake troll, and judging by its comment, that was exactly what the creature had in mind. The Psychic's scolding of the lake troll after his expressed concern was further proof (at least for me) that I would be gobbled up by this thing if it had a chance.

"Are we gonna talk, or are we gonna get on with this?" I challenged. I wish I felt as confident as I managed to sound in that moment.

"In a hurry to be my servant, ghoul?" Blumegastrickfiggernilly chortled. I hate when the bad guy does that. And seriously, I was feeling pretty confident after taking down those ogres.

"I still say you should just leave her to me," a familiar voice hissed.

I was really curious how the Psychic was pulling off this little stunt where the voices seemed to be coming from every side. This was keeping me from knowing the general direction to his location.

"And I have explained to you that she is quite useful if—" and then it went silent. I mean, there was still the normal sloshing sound of the lake troll as it shifted on its feet while we sort of circled each other, but the Psychic's voice simply stopped.

"Looks like it is just you and me, kid," I muttered.

The lake troll cocked its head to one side. My first thought was that it had heard me and was trying to puzzle my comment. Then I heard it too. They came in a rush, and as soon as they reached the edge of the parking lot, Nose Wart and his band of goblins—short a few members if my count was correct—came rushing into the lot with their tiny swords waving wildly.

"So this is what it feels like to be saved by the cavalry." I smiled as the lake troll suddenly seemed unsure. He turned to face this new threat and then glanced over his shoulder at me. Wait…why is he smiling?

Then I got my answer.

In one massive scoop he gathered up the charging goblins and popped them in his mouth like so many Tic Tacs! The emotions swirled in me and fought for top billing as I felt anger and sadness in equal parts. I had loved those little disgusting creatures. With my own scream of rage, I charged.

The lake troll was making some sort of sick gulping sound. I forced my mind to not think of poor Nose Wart and the others.

Noooo! a voice wailed in my head.

Great, just what I needed right now, a hysterical goblin in my brain. I tried to force her back to confinement, but apparently her sorrow and anger were too much.

Kill it! Kill that horrible thing! Butt Pimple snarled with a rage that made her sound very much like her old goblin self again. As the lake troll threw its head back and made one last show of swallowing, I took my chance.

Coming in low, I brought my switchfingers in a roundhouse swipe at the massive oak tree-sized legs of the lake troll. They sliced through like a hot knife through butter. I was feeling pretty good about it until a massive hand came down and scooped me up. The lake troll seemed unaffected by my attack.

"Crap," I managed as I shot up like I was in an express elevator.

If it was not happening to me personally, it might have been almost comical. There I was, my arms now pinned to my sides as the lake troll held me like a knock off Barbie doll. Yeah, that would just about cover the size difference.

I don't know what I had been thinking when I had even the slightest glimmer of a thought that I could fight something like this and win…or even survive.

As the lake troll opened its massive mouth, I swear that I

saw bits of goblin limbs stuck between its teeth. I would have shuddered if there had been time. Instead, I was suddenly catapulted forward like a contestant being launched into the Wipeout Zone at the end of that crazy obstacle course game show. However, instead of a pool of cold water, it was the cavernous mouth of the lake troll.

I bounced off of something that may have been a tonsil…and then the lake troll slammed its mouth shut.

That Ghoul Ava…On the Lam!

15

Ride the Lightning

"Dammit!" I cursed as I landed on the spongy and disgusting tongue of the lake troll.

Then it was like a massive earthquake as I was being shifted around. I was being forced towards those horrendous teeth. A thought bloomed and I decided to go with it. It was very "spur of the moment" and I had no time to come up with something elaborate—or any more likely to succeed.

I threw myself to the back of the creature's throat.

For a second or two, it was like a freefall. When I reached a point where things got cozy, I was upside down. Something squeezed me tight and then I was forced downward again.

I could actually hear the steady and slow pounding of the creature's heart. I would have been more amazed if I was not totally scared out of my wits.

That scene in *Star Wars* when Jabba is about to sacrifice Luke and Han to that nasty open maw that looked very much like something you would see in an inappropriately close picture in *Hustler* magazine came to mind. Threepio had said something about how they were about to be digested over a thousand years or some such nonsense.

Then I heard it. At first I thought that I might be imagining things. Then I heard it again.

"When I get out of here I am going to slice off your hemorrhoids and then force them down your throat!"

"Nose Wart?" I called.

"Is that you, Just Ava?" came the reply. "Now my failure is complete. I have failed to protect you in your battle and now you suffer a fate not worthy of a hairless bugbear with explosive diarrhea!"

I was about to make a comment when another forceful constriction sent me plunging downwards once more. I landed with an ungraceful splash in the foulest smelling goop I have ever had the displeasure to inhale.

I came up spitting and sputtering. The stuff was thicker than water, but not quite as thick as that green crap they are always dumping on people on that Nickelodeon channel. It tingled and I could only assume that this was the stomach acid of the lake troll.

Then a new smell hit me. It was something yummy. My eyes scanned and I discovered the partially masticated corpse of about a third of what had once been a goblin. Oh well, beggars can't be choosers.

It wasn't terrible, but that coating of lake troll tummy juice was no ketchup. After I rummaged about, I discovered a few more choice bits and made them learn what a real stomach was like.

I wiped my mouth and turned to see three goblins standing hobbled on the far side of what, by logical deduction, had to be the stomach of the lake troll. Nose Wart was just to their right and watching me with a little bit of concern.

"Sorry, were those friends of yours?" I asked meekly.

"They live and die to serve you, Just Ava. You have done them a great honor," Nose Wart replied. I glanced at the trio and did not think they shared his sentiment.

"So, you guys are sort of the Supernatural corn in the lake troll's diet," I quipped. Unfortunately that joke sailed right over their heads.

Looking around, I was fighting the feeling of revulsion as my eyes took in the pinkish and gray walls of slime that were laced with black veins.

"So this is the inside of a lake troll," I muttered as I sloshed around, getting a better look at my surroundings. At one point, I stepped on something knobby and sort of circular. I had a feeling that was the "natural" exit. I would not want to leave that way. Just the thought made me want to laugh and be sick at the same time.

"We will perish slowly, Just Ava," Nose Wart said as he came to stand beside me. "I would be honored if you eat me to sustain yourself."

I glanced down at the goblin. All of a sudden, he was no longer the cute puppy that I had started to see him as; instead, he had reverted to his original warrior version that I had first met. He had his arms folded across his chest and he was inspecting the surroundings like he anticipated battle at some point soon.

I resisted the urge to pat him on the head. After all, he had just basically given me the go ahead to kill and eat him in order to survive longer. The thing is, I did not plan on ever taking him up on that offer. Another new idea was brewing.

Suddenly, a loud, sonorous noise started. I had to put my hands over my ears to shut out enough so that it did not feel like my head was splitting down the middle. It took me a few minutes, but I finally realized what it was, the lake troll was talking. I could not make out the words, but I recognized the pattern of speech. It sort of reminded me of if Metallica was cranked to full blast but the vocals were done by the teacher from the Charlie Brown cartoons.

It seemed to go on for quite a while, but if you are being subjected to unpleasant sounds at insane decibels, I imagine it feels longer than it truly is in reality. It was like when this one guy I dated took me out to dinner. We got in his car and his radio was on a country station. The trip was maybe twenty minutes, but it was the longest twenty minutes of my life; and then the poor guy didn't score that night either, because the trip back to my place was almost as bad of a mood killer than if he'd had chronic garlic flatulence.

At long last, the sound died down. The goblins had settled

in with expressions of grim determination. They were actually prepared for the long slow death that they imagined to be their fate. Well, I had a surprise in store for them, or at least I hoped that I did.

I tromped over to the wall of the stomach and gave it a little poke with one regular finger. It was disgusting and felt like what I remember raw liver feeling like. (And don't start on the thing about me eating dead people whole, I am relating to an old human memory that will hopefully make sense to you and give you a better understanding of what I am dealing with at the moment.)

"What are you doing, Just Ava?' a goblin asked.

I turned and was surprised to see that it was not Nose Wart. One of the trio had approached me. This was out of the ordinary because, since they'd been residents at my home, Nose Wart had been the only one of the goblins to actually speak with me directly. The rest always hung back or flat out hid from me.

That is Twiggle, Butt Pimple said, suddenly at the forefront of my consciousness.

Twiggle? I asked. It almost seemed odd. Goblins had gross, funny names that had to do with body parts and the ugly ailments that plague them.

He is too young to have a proper name. That must be earned.

I was not going to ask about the finer details on claiming what was considered by goblins to be a proper name. Instead, I returned my attention to the goblin standing beside me.

"I have a plan," I told the goblin. "One that will hopefully get us out of here."

My excellent vision made it easy to see the brief expression of relief that crossed the goblin's features. I think I knew who was to be first on my menu.

"Perhaps you would like to help," I offered.

The goblin looked at me with open incredulity. Just how high up on the chain did these goblins see me?

You are like a goddess for them, Butt Pimple told me. I noticed that she said "them" instead of "us." I might have to explore things with my new mental resident at a later time. For now, I had a few more pressing matters on my docket.

"I am honored to serve, Just Ava," Twiggle said, and then prostrated himself right there in the stomach juices of the lake troll.

"First, get up," I told him, trying not to be totally grossed out by the goo that cascaded off of him when he did as I'd instructed. "Second, do you have your sword handy?"

Twiggle pulled his rusty looking blade free from its sheath and held it out to me. I eased his hand down and turned him towards the wall lining of this cavernous stomach bag.

"Cut the wall." I thought that my instructions were clear enough. Yet, the goblin looked at me like I had grown a second head or something.

"Twiggle, this is nothing more than a belly. I am sure that you have cut open a belly or two." The goblin nodded fiercely.

"I slayed five of the vile Cow Fart goblins just this very evening. One of them disgraced himself by begging for mercy as I drove my blade through and spilled his innards to the ground. I laughed while I ate his insides and then pissed on his cold corpse before leaving him for the bugs to finish."

"Uh-huh." What else was I going to say to that? I suppressed a small shiver at the thought of this goblin eating the guts of another of his kind a mere hour or two ago. "Well, good for you." It took me a few seconds to get my brain to circle back to the reason that I'd been talking to him in the first place. "So, can you use your sword to cut right here?" I tapped a spot on the stomach wall.

I know some people hate when I go off on a tangent, but can I just say that there is nothing in life that you can compare to when trying to describe being inside a stomach. There are smells, and sounds. Oh yeah, and I bet you hadn't even thought about what it must be like on the inside when your tummy is growling. Well, go check out the web site called "How Stuff Works" and read about why your stomach growls. This entire time, I had to keep moving in order to not lose my balance and fall into the murk that is sloshing around my legs all the way to the shin.

Twiggle drew his sword and then, after a look over his shoulder at me to get a nod of approval, he drove his sword into the slimy meat of the lake troll's stomach bag. There was a hiss and a whole new batch of smells, but he managed to make a cut about a foot long before there was a massive heave and we all went tumbling.

"That had to hurt!" I yelled.

Unfortunately, Twiggle's sword snapped off at the hilt. Even worse, now we were being thrown around like rocks in a dryer. It was very unpleasant, let's just leave it at that.

Then I slapped my forehead with my palm. I had been on a roll with some pretty good ideas lately. After all, coming here had been part of my master plan. Sure, I had not counted on being eaten by a lake troll, but other than that, things were going perfectly.

Sort of.

Mostly.

Okay, not so great, but I had a better plan now.

Snick.

I went at it like the Tasmanian Devil. Switchfingers and toes began to shred the inside of the stomach of the lake troll. I saw a wall of dark purples and grays that had all this gooey yellowish stuff clinging to it and went crazy. That was the last layer—the belly of the lake troll—and I tore it to ribbons, my reward being a rush of fresh night air that hit me with more effect than the sweetest smells of the freshest corpse. Okay, that probably is not something that you equate to yummy or wonderful, but you have been with me long enough to understand and insert your own metaphors.

I was just barely out of the belly of the lake troll when a few dozen goblins rushed in with their little swords raised. I heard a bunch of chatter in what had to be goblin, but I did not need a translator to know what they were basically saying. It was something to the effect of, "Kill the ghoul!"

They picked the wrong day. I was not very happy considering the fact that I was covered in lake troll stomach juice. Oh, and I had four goblins as my backup. I think it was Twiggle that actually shoved me aside to meet the charge. In any case, the fight only lasted a minute or so. I was spinning and slashing with my switchdigits alongside Nose Wart and company as we took down what proved to be the last of the Cow Fart clan.

I had a few nicks and slices, so my initial reaction was to scoop up the corpses and gobble them up to expedite my healing. That was not to be the case.

Stop! Butt Pimple shrieked as I held the first body up to my mouth. It was really little more than a snack that would be gone in one bite, but that scream caused my teeth to snap shut like a bear trap. *You cannot eat that body.*

Umm, actually I can, I replied mentally. *Wanna see?*

That is their leader. If you consume him, he will join me in here.

So? I was still in the throes of my battle lust or I probably would have figured it out on my own.

As the clan leader, he is considered powerful in the Supernatural realm, Ava, Blodwen spoke up. *He would become a new resident here in your mind. His hatred for the queen of the Castrated Mallard clan would be a natural source of animosity. These two would be at each other's throats constantly. The battle skills he might pass on would be negligible compared to the, excuse the pun, headache.*

He would not have been the first unruly denizen of my mind, but I saw her point. I did not need to complicate my life. Besides, there were plenty of other corpses lying about.

I turned to Twiggle. "You want to eat this guy?"

The other goblins all froze. Twiggle instantly fell to his belly and started to sound like Wayne and Garth with all the cries of how unworthy he was for such an honor.

"Look, you helped cut our way out of that lake troll's belly," I grabbed him by the shoulder and pulled him to his feet. "You earned this."

I know that I did most of the work, but I really did not see the big deal. Besides, I heard something coming at a run and had a feeling that I would have my hands full in a minute. I just wanted to wolf down a couple of my own dead goblins and be at full strength by the time that this new threat arrived on the scene.

The other goblins had gathered around. Nose Wart was actually staring open-mouthed at me. I was suddenly concerned that I had violated some silly goblin code and that I would be attacked by my own minions.

You have given Twiggle the ultimate honor, Butt Pimple breathed in apparent awe. *You have offered him the corpse of the fallen leader. That is a prize reserved for only the bravest and most valiant warriors.*

The goblins all dropped to the ground beside Twiggle and took up the chant of how they were unworthy dogs and other more creative cries that I did not have time for. Did I mention that I heard something approaching, and I was willing to bet that it was not friendly?

"We can do this later," I snapped. "Twiggle, eat this thing and everybody get ready, a new foe is approaching fast from the woods."

Surprisingly, that proved good enough. Twiggle tore into the dead goblin king's corpse and I grabbed a few of the other bodies and scarfed them down like I was expecting my date to arrive any minute now to take me to dinner.

What? Am I the only one of you ladies out there that did that? And, fellas, that is so cute that you believe we don't have a very big appetite. The reason we don't eat much of what we order is because we are trying to make you see us as dainty and delicate flowers to be treated with gentle delicateness. Not that it works even half the time. All that pawing and groping? Can I just say that your having bought dinner does not guarantee you a trip to the Magic Kingdom? I don't care how much that lobster dinner cost. We are worth a helluva lot more than whatever you paid for dinner and a few drinks.

I had just gulped down the second dead goblin when the trees on the far side of the pond were shoved aside like a shower curtain. I only had a moment to wonder how that might be explained to the mortal humans of the area. There was no storm to blame it on, but that was just one of my passing thoughts as I set my feet and prepared for the charging giant that stomped across the pond. He was not much bigger than the lake troll, but since that had not ended well, I was understandably concerned.

"A mountain giant," Nose Wart muttered with a dismissive snort. "They aren't so tough."

This one sure looked tough to me.

I did a quick seek, looking for any signs of that bastard, Blumegastrickfiggernilly. I was really hoping that I could get my hands on him before the night was over. Rules be damned, I wanted to shred him to ribbons. And there was no power on earth that would force me to take his district as the regional Psychic.

My seek was cut short as the giant roared a challenge and charged. I smiled. That was almost too easy. He came in with all the overconfidence of a schoolyard bully. Kids, take a tip from your Aunt Ava; if a bully is giving you grief. Punch them right in the nose. Don't tell them you are gonna do it. Just haul off and belt them. Yes, I realize that flies in the face of conventional (and often ridiculous) New Age parenting advice. I am not much for these modern times.

Have we met?

The giant closed the gap in three strides and lifted what I am pretty sure was an entire pine tree that had been stripped of its branches. He thought he was going to end this fight in one stroke. I waited until the last possible second and then dove forward. I came up just behind his left ankle. One swipe and that tendon was severed.

The giant went to his knees and howled in pain. I did not give him a chance to do anything. I leaped to the other ankle that was now outstretched behind him as the giant had dropped to the ground from the crippling strike landed by yours truly. A second swipe ensured that he would never regain his footing.

The goblins were not about to be left out of this little fight. They charged in and began stabbing with their swords or biting and clawing. I don't really think the giant noticed, but it made them feel better, I imagine.

Another leap had me on the giant's shoulder. "Time to die," I whispered in one massive ear. And then I drove my switchfingers into the temple.

"Too easy," I scoffed as I leapt free of the body just before it collapsed with a meaty slap on the ground.

"That the best you got?" I called into the darkness.

"Actually, that would be me," a voice hissed from behind.

I spun to see Sheila the lamia slither over the top of the dead body of the lake troll. I willed my claws to retract for a moment and my hand went into my pocket. I brought out the phone just enough to see the button that would call Morgan's witch. I thumbed the call button, and then shoved the phone back into my pocket. I heard it pick up on the first ring. That was comforting.

"Come to take me on now that I am softened up?" I asked.

Actually, I was simply stalling for time. I was getting a good look at this horrible creature. The first time, it had been so chaotic that I had not really given her a full head-to-toe inspection. Okay, lamias don't have toes, but you get my meaning. It had been superficial at best; more about sizing up my opponent. This time, I was taking in the details.

Those clawed out eye sockets were more than a little disturbing. The fact that she had done that to herself was an extra heaping of creepy.

"I am surprised to see you here after last time." Sheila slithered closer. There was still a good distance between us, but I brought the switchfingers back and prepared for her to charge at any moment. "And you brought me some more treats." Her gaze flicked to the goblins standing to either side of me.

"Was it worth it?" I asked. That seemed to catch her off guard.

"Was what worth it?" The lamia halted and her head cocked to one side. I found that gesture just a bit creepy considering her empty sockets were locked on to me like she could actually see.

"Becoming this horrid creature just so you could screw some married guy, get him to leave his wife and kids, and then knock you up with a baby that you would never lay eyes on."

The lamia recoiled as if struck. That made me feel good. At least I knew that she felt something. My mental victory was short lived as she came back with a comment of her own.

"How is your little Templar bitch?" Sheila crooned in a way that told me she knew damn good and well how Lisa had fared.

"She would have joined us, but she was a little tied up." Sure, I know that was sort of the cheap and easy way to reply, but I think I have commented in the past that my retorts are not usually as witty as what you might find in some of those action films.

"She still lives?" At first I did not realize that had been posed as a question. Once I did, I smiled.

"She is very much alive and well," I lied. Okay, it was not exactly a lie, but it was far from the truth.

"Interesting."

The lamia began to circle me, and I knew that our little chit chat was basically over. It was time to get down to the business of trying to kill each other. I sure hoped that this spell thingy worked through the phone. Of course I also hoped that I did not die in the process. I was in no way confident that I could survive this fight if the lamia set her mind to killing me.

The goblins spread out. I was confident that they knew better than to try to bite this thing. Also, they should be aware of the effects of that nasty tail stinger that had regenerated.

She made the first move as our circling of each other brought us closer and closer. The tail came around like a whip and missed my head by less than an inch. On reflex, I brought my claws around and just nicked her. I felt the instant pain as her blood began to fizz on my digits.

The goblins charged suddenly and with mixed results. I saw Twiggle fall back, his hand sending up tendrils of smoke as the flesh was eaten away after his claw attack struck home and the blood began to do its dirty work.

"Twiggle, drop back!" I snapped as I moved in with the vial palmed and ready.

"I shall gladly die in your service, Just Ava!" the little goblin barked in response as he charged in once more and took a swipe with his one remaining good hand. Maybe his goblin name could be Gnarled Stubbyhands.

The lamia spun her torso to face Nose Wart. My intrepid little goblin friend raised his sword in defense as she lunged in to try and bite him. I only had a second to marvel as he parried her attack and rolled underneath one of her coils. Popping up, he drove his blade down, plunging it into the scaly flesh. The blood welled up, but Nose Wart was already scurrying away before any of it could splash on him.

The lamia screamed in agony. This was my chance.

I leapt up and landed on her back. It had almost no effect on her, but her head craned around and I saw her mouth curve in an evil smile. When the tail struck me, I hardly felt a thing. Her expression of malice melted into one of confusion.

"You are not supposed to be able to resist my poison! Ghouls are not immune!" Sheila ranted.

You are more than just a ghoul, Ava, Blodwen's voice filtered in to me from somewhere deep within my mind. *That is her mistake, now finish her!*

I brought the vial up and flipped the top with my thumb. I was not shoving my hand down her throat this time. Using an old trick that I had used on my pets when giving them a pill they did not want to eat, I pinched her nose, poured the fluid in her mouth, and then forced her mouth shut.

"It is in!" I yelled, hoping that the phone had not disconnected in all the action.

A tinny voice began to chant. The lamia started to buck wildly, and I ended up being tossed several feet to land gracelessly in the open parking lot. I rolled and came to my knees, ready for anything. Well, almost anything.

The lamia was thrashing around and I could see her body seeming to eat itself as if her toxic blood had suddenly become too much for her to handle. I was watching with morbid fascination as she dissolved before my very eyes.

I guess that was why I did not see the van until it came to a stop about twenty feet away. The doors opened and five individuals emerged from it dressed in full battle gear that gave them away as being Templar.

"Ava Birch, you will come with us!" a woman said, stepping forward and drawing what looked like a seriously modified old flintlock style pistol.

"Umm, no." Pretty witty comeback, huh?

Actually, that seemed to befuddle the little Templar gang for a moment. I saw two options at that particular instant in time. I could run...or fight. I was still making up my mind when a thought blossomed; whether it was my own or inspired from one of my mental denizens, I was not certain.

"Who sent you?" I challenged.

"That is not important, ghoul," the Templar finally replied after glancing at her cohorts and getting slight nods in response.

"Actually, it is important."

"Are you going to come peacefully, or do we have to do this in a much less pleasant way?" The female Templar brought her weapon up and aimed it at me.

I took a step back, my eyes scanning each one and discovering that they all had one of those funky looking weapons. I had a feeling they were meant specifically for ghouls and that if I got a chance to look at one, I would see the Blue Steel logo stamped on it somewhere.

"And what exactly brought you all the way out here?" I asked, edging back slowly.

"We received an anonymous tip," the woman replied after seeming to consider my question as well as her answer.

"She is mine," another voice spoke.

Well, I thought, *that blows the theory of who I suspected gave the anonymous tip*.

Blumegastrickfiggernilly appeared to literally materialize out of the shadows. And that was weird since I don't have any problems with seeing in darkness. He strode out to a spot that sort of put us in a triangle.

Wah-uh-wah-uh-waaah! My mind conjured up the theme from *The Good, The Bad, and the Ugly*. When a woman appeared on Blumegastrickfiggernilly's arm from those same mystical shadows, the tune finished. *Wah-wah-wahhhh.*

"And who might you be?" the woman challenged.

"Interesting," the Psychic mused. "If you were truly a Templar, you would know exactly who I am. So, that begs the question. Who are *you* really?"

Uh-oh. This was all going over my head. I had fake Templars with peculiar weapons, a mysterious woman who was way too hot to be slumming with old Blue—Psychic or not.

Beware the woman, Blodwen warned. *Magic is leaking from her in a way that is not natural.*

I could argue later that magic by nature was not something you could consider normal. Still, I heeded the warning and kept more of my attention on her.

As I did, I was able to get a better look at this woman.

She was super-hot, which I think I already mentioned. She was a light mocha with straight black hair that came to the midpoint of her back. Her eyes were a dazzling purple. Okay, not a normal eye color, I know. But I was willing to wager that they were not contact lenses. She had amazing lips that were painted a ruby red. She sort of reminded me of Vanessa Williams. Not the skanky version that got smeared in Penthouse. No, I am talking about the pageant winner and singer that I knew.

Then, all hell broke loose. People started shooting, and the hot woman beside Blue did this crazy gesture with her hands that caused a shimmering dome of radiant purple light (that matched her eyes) to spring up around her and Blumegastrickfiggernilly. The rounds fired from those guns were not bullets, of that I was certain when the first black projectile whizzed past and hit that force field or whatever.

For one, they moved much slower than a bullet; I would say just a bit faster than a major leaguer's fastball. They crackled with energy, and when they hit that force field, silver sparks raced across the surface. If I had to guess, I would say that they were some sort of energy ball.

I did the only thing that I could think of: I ran.

I dove behind a tree just as one of those projectiles clipped me in the leg. The pain was instant and complete. In other words, while I was barely grazed on the calf, I felt it all the way to my fingertips. It was like standing in a mud puddle while being hit by a bolt of lightning.

The bad news was that I could not even move for several seconds. It felt like my entire body seized up and went rigid. I had to wait a few blinks of the eyes before I started to loosen up. The good news was that these Templar impersonators were busy, as the witch was summoning down her own firestorm from the sky.

I made it to my hands and knees eventually and took a moment to assess the situation. Then the other van arrived. The group that poured out of it was dressed much like the other group, but they did not have funky guns. Instead, they wore a jangling arsenal of blades and bludgeons—with one exception. This guy was the human equivalent of the ultimate action figure with the butt of a rifle jutting over each shoulder and some sort of landscape leveling machine gun on his hip.

I peeked up in time to watch the Templar version of Rambo mow down the fake Templars with that massive machine gun. Apparently that was more than Blue and his witch wanted to deal with, because I saw them vanish in a flash of bright blue light.

"Ava Birch!" a voice bellowed. "Come out or this will go poorly for you."

"And why would I do that?" I shouted back.

"Because, if you do not, then we will be forced to kill you here without your having the benefit of a proper trial," one of the real Templars (at least I think they are real) called back.

While that seemed like a good reason, I was not going to surrender just so I could be tried and then hung—or however they planned on executing me. Honestly, I think we all know there was no way I would be getting anything that resembled a fair trial.

"Then I guess you better start shooting!" I called out.

I winced as the words left my mouth, but after being bashed by ogres, swallowed by a lake troll, ambushed by goblins, charged by a mountain giant, facing down a lamia, and then attacked by fake Templars with colonial space weapons, I guess I'd had enough. And that returns us to the beginning.

That Ghoul Ava…On the Lam!

16

Jump

The bullets flew in a hailstorm of angry lead bees. Yep, that just about covers it. All I could do at the moment was lie flat on my stomach and let them shoot themselves out. It wasn't so much that I was worried about being killed. I seriously doubted that the Templars had managed to manufacture special ghoul-killing rounds. However, I did not want to be injured to the point where I would require *Fame Rabia* to recover.

I saw the goblins hunkered down as well. They looked as annoyed as I felt.

"You guys head home, I'll catch up," I told Nose Wart over the epic buzz of the massive machine gun.

"Our place is at your side," Nose Wart said with a shake of the head. "We will fight with you to the end."

"I think the fighting is done. I am out of here the first chance I get. I don't want to have to worry about you guys. Now do as I say!"

And that was all it took. Nose Wart gave an abrupt nod of the head. He, Twiggle, and all the others took off into the shadows. Now it was just me. Well…me and the Templars.

I had been on my belly for a few seconds when it came to me. Didn't some hero always say "Cover me!" to his pals and then rush the foxhole or whatever?

"Ah crap!" I managed to mutter just as I heard the bushes being trampled by the designated hero.

I rolled to one side just as a sword plunged into the ground where I'd been lying just a second ago. Now that was a weapon with ghoul eradicating ability.

"What did I ever do to you guys," I snarled as I was able to jump up now that the hail of gunfire from the mountainous Templar action figure ceased.

The Templar that had been sent in (or charged in to try and be a hero) had the courtesy to look befuddled. He held his sword across his body in a defensive stance and was now trying to move in a direction that I had to imagine would put me in the open and subject me once more to that Gatling gun that had taken down a nice sized section of the woods that bordered this side of the parking lot.

I only had a few moments to consider why not one single human had come on the scene during all of this. I realized this was a small town, and that farms were the primary source of employment—except for the Tillamook Cheese Factory, of course.

"You are a ghoul," the Templar sputtered his answer as if that were really all that needed to be said on the subject.

"And what does that mean, *exactly*," I pressed.

The Templar just stared at me with absolute confusion. I had to liken it to the poor children who grow up in the family of white supremacists (or black ones for that matter…supremacism of any sort is appalling in my book). If you ask them why they hate, they can parrot the doctrines, but they are truly parrots in the sense that they are just saying words with no actual knowledge of what it is they are saying.

"You are the imbalance, you are the creature that will send humanity to its doom."

He said it with such conviction that I was almost convinced. And, clearly, he believed this mantra to his core. But at least now I was being told what they taught the Templars. Lisa and Race would never divulge such things to me; whether it was out of some misguided effort to protect my feelings, or perhaps just because they did not want to have their little ideology mocked and ridiculed. Whatever the reason, they had never shared this "party" line with me about the Templar hatred for the ghoul.

Okay, to be fair, they are mostly concerned with a female ghoul. After all, we can absorb and take on the powers of some of the Supernaturals that we consume. That turns us into a pretty badass weapon. I guess I am like what nuclear weapons were back in that glorious Decade of Decadence—the 80s. Back when Ronny was a cowboy staring down the Kremlin and demanding that Gorby "tear down this wall."

I am the scary thing.

The ender of the world.

"I am actually going to give you the chance to walk away," I finally said with a sigh.

I seriously doubted that he or the other Templar sheep would accept my more than generous offer. This kid was itching to put a notch in his holster; and not the cool sexual metaphor version. Nope, he wanted me dead.

"Cut her down!" a voice bellowed from across the lot.

"We are trying to have a conversation here!" I yelled back.

I was beginning to think that this kid had not so much charged in to be a hero as I imagined that he was the one who drew the short straw. He was a Templar redshirt! (And if you did not just get that joke, you have my pity.)

Well, I was not about to give these guys the monster that they craved. I must be maturing.

Naaaaaw!

Shut up, Blodwen, I snarked.

"Some other time, sweetie," I cooed. And then, after darting in and kissing his cheek before he had the chance to react, I sprung backwards with all I was worth.

I had jumped a few times in the recent past and bumped my head on a low ceiling. And by low, I am talking twenty or thirty feet. To date, I had never tried to vault with all my strength. I was not expecting Hulk or Superman abilities, but I was thinking that I would get some good air. I was right.

I landed on the other side of the pond and a good fifty feet or so back in the woods. In all the excitement, I had lost track of time. A sudden surge of panic hit me until I realized that I had the phone. I pulled it out and swiped the screen. It was only three in the morning. I still had plenty of time to get home. The only problem was how to accomplish that feat.

Almost on cue, the generic melody that acted as the default ringtone sounded. It showed up as "Unknown Caller" on the screen.

"Hello?" I answered, curious as to who I would have on the other end.

"Ava, meet us at the ship in front of the cheese factory." *Click.* And that was it. Better than nothing, I guess.

Deciding to put my jumping skills through a bit of a shake-down, I leapt again and again until I came down in the middle of the golf course that is across the street from the Tillamook Cheese Factory. From here, it was just a short jog. I kept on high alert, but nothing nasty showed up.

Don't you just hate in the horror movies where there always has to be a second killing of the monster? I mean, ever since Jason came up out of that lake or Michael vanished at the end, Hollywood has taken that idea and gone crazy. Well, no worries here.

I reached the parking lot and the Hummer that I had been dropped off from was sitting all by itself, idling and waiting with the door open.

I jumped in and was greeted by Race turning around from the driver's seat. "The lamia?"

"Dead," I said with a nod.

"Good, now let's get out of here. I saw a Templar van shoot past a few minutes ago." Race turned out of the lot and started back toward home.

I could not stop looking out the back. I really did expect any moment to see the headlights of a van appear. They would fol-low us and we would have to race along the winding mountain road until we were door-to-door, slamming into each other. Eventually, one of us (them hopefully) would be launched through a guardrail and tumble down a mountain ravine until they hit the ground and exploded in a huge ball of fire. Then, somebody would say something clever and we would all laugh. The credits would roll and the screen would start to shrink in on itself until it paused on just my face where I would wink, flash my winning smile, and blow a kiss.

"Ava!" Morgan snapped.

"Huh?" I shook my head to clear it.

I hadn't spaced out that bad in a while. I looked around to see that we were already almost out of Portland and turning on to the highway that led to Estacada. A light rain was falling and washing away that little bit of snow that remained; so much for a white Christmas.

"You're hurt," the Psychic said with an uncommon gentleness in her voice.

I told them about the weapon and that it had only clipped my leg. I looked down and was surprised to discover that there was no outward sign of injury. Not even any damage to my clothes.

"Pull over," Morgan ordered.

Race did it without question. I didn't see the big deal. And just like that, I was falling. Only...not.

I looked around and saw a room decorated in posters of Brett and the boys. Sitting on a couch were Blodwen and Butt Pimple. They seemed surprised when I apparently materialized out of thin air.

"Oh dear!" Blodwen climbed to her feet and rushed over to me.

I looked down to see what was causing her such alarm and was surprised to see that my entire leg looked like a log on a campfire. It was all charcoal black, but you could see the orange of fire licking up through the cracks in my skin.

"That can't be good."

And then I passed out.

***

I drifted in and out, but each time I came to, the pain was

more than I could handle. I remember screaming and passing out more than once. It seemed that any time I "came to" during this episode, I was unable to go to my happy little Ava Land and block out the pain.

But, all good (or bad) things must come to an end. And that was the case here. One day I simply opened my eyes and found myself staring up at the bare walls of my mind. I only had to make a mental adjustment and the 80s deco was back. I turned to see Blodwen standing at my side.

"Welcome back," Blodwen said with a genuine smile.

"We thought you might not make it," Butt Pimple added, stepping up beside the gwyll.

"How long?" I asked as I sat up.

"In here it is too difficult to tell," a male voice said from behind me.

I whipped my head around and was stunned to discover Mystify. Only, he was nothing like I remembered. This was an emaciated old man. His clothing was little more than rags which allowed me to see the knobs on his back. He looked like a cross between a human and a stegosaurus. Only, instead of plates, it was a row of bulbed, mushroom-looking knobs.

"What is he doing out?" I asked, easing off the table that had served as my bed.

"We needed him," Blodwen said with a dismissive wave. "And since I trusted Adrianna even less than I do this one, he got a temporary reprieve."

"Put him back in his room," I said with an unveiled threat ringing in my voice. "I don't know exactly what you have started and set into motion, but all of this is somehow your fault. I can't prove anything yet, but one day, the big Scooby Doo reveal is going to happen. And when it does, if I have to drag Adrianna out and make her show me, I will rid myself of you for good."

Actually, I did not know how he was even standing here. I thought he'd been dispatched by the aforementioned Queen of the Zombies.

To his credit, Mystify did nothing more than bow and return to the door that led to his room or cell or whatever you want to call it. As soon as the door shut, a terrible black goop seeped from the walls and covered the door.

I turned back to Blodwen and flashed an awkward, if not apologetic, smile. "I really do appreciate all you did…whatever you did to get me fixed."

"Oh, dearie, you are far from fixed. Whatever that was that they hit you with, it drains your energy constantly. Unfed, you will slip into *Fame Rabia* every twelve hours or so." Blodwen's grim expression made me believe that she had led with the good news. "You will not be able to mindwalk again until you can find a way to counteract what has been done to you. And if you slip into *Fame Rabia* without being able to Mindwalk and block out or even ease the pain, you might go on a killing spree that will end poorly not only for you, but also for the entire Supernatural community."

"Like the lamia," I said with a sigh.

"Much worse."

I dropped my head. This was getting to be too much. I needed to get out of my head and fix whatever had been done to me. The biggest problem was that I had no idea how to even begin.

"I guess I better get moving."

I shut my eyes and pictured that long, dark hallway. The rectangle of light was inviting and warm looking. I stepped through and felt myself shift or fall or float or whatever the hell I did when I returned to my body proper.

"Ava?" Lisa's voice was sweet music to my ears.

I had almost forgotten how I'd left her the last time we'd been together. Actually, that is not true. 'Almost" is a lie. I had completely forgotten.

I opened my eyes and was pleased to find her standing beside my bed. She had some scarring on her face and a nasty scab on her neck, but she did not look like she wanted to kill me or say a bunch of mean things.

I reached over with my free hand and patted the one of hers that was holding mine. She gave me a squeeze and a smile.

"Glad to see you are okay," I said.

"And we are glad to see that you are fine as well," Morgan's voice came from somewhere. I had to crane my neck and arch my back to see her. That was also when I discovered that I was secured to the bed.

"What the hell happened?" I asked. Things were fuzzy and almost like a dream. There was a part of me that was seriously hoping that was the case.

"An extremist faction of the Templars have apparently developed a new weapon," Race's voice chimed in.

Jeez, was this a freakin' party? And considering how long I had likely been strapped down, I bet I had a hideous case of bed hair.

"It would seem that they are aligned with a group of radical Psychics." Edward moved up beside Race almost in a universal effort to complete my embarrassment.

"This is all well and good, but can I be let loose now?" I grumped. "And could everybody kindly give me some privacy so that I can get cleaned up." That last bit was not a question, although it was sort of predicated on the answer to my actual question.

"Actually, I have to be going," Race said. He came over to my bed and put a hand on my shoulder. "It would seem that there is about to be some big changes on the horizon. Why am I not surprised that you are apparently going to be at its center?"

"And I will be going with him," Edward added, but he did not come over to me. Instead, he gave Morgan a very business-like handshake. "I will be in touch. I believe that the council will be summoning you within the week."

"And I have some things that must be attended to before…" Morgan stopped and shot me a curious look. She came over beside me and took my hand. "You are going to be fine, Ava. We will see to it. I have every witch in two states, independent and otherwise, working on the problem." She gave my hand a pat and headed up the stairs with the two men, leaving me alone with Lisa.

"Is she going to be okay?" a gravelly voice whispered once everybody was gone.

"Twiggle!" I was glad that the goblins had made it home as

he, Nose Wart, and the other two stepped up beside the bed.

"My name is Belly Ulcer," the little goblin said proudly. "I have been given my clan name."

"Good for you." I was genuinely happy for the little guy.

Lisa undid the straps that held me in place and helped me to my feet. She didn't even leave the room when I fed. I guess she'd been through enough *Fame Rabias* to get over whatever squeamishness that she might have had.

"Where is Aoife?" I asked, realizing that this little reunion was still missing some key elements.

"Betty called last night and said that she will probably not be able to leave the island for at least a few more months. She barely survived."

I recalled her story about the island of her origin. I tried to tell myself that she was in good hands and that she would be okay. As for Betty being the one to call in, when I questioned Lisa, she said that Betty probably won't be back for another year or so. Apparently she has been recruited by Morgan to rally some Supernatural reinforcements. It was only then that I realized that I had not seen her since returning from Dallas.

"Things aren't going to get any easier, are they?" I asked as I finished my meal and flopped down on the couch.

"No, I don't think they are," Lisa sighed as she plopped down beside me.

I made it a point to just enjoy this simple moment. I had a feeling that they would be scarce for the foreseeable future.

Step into the DEAD world created by TW Brown -
Follow along with the DEAD - the 12 book series starting with
The Ugly Beginning - or enjoy a few laughs following Ava
Birch's adventures in the horror/comedy That Ghoul Ava

MAY DECEMBER
Publications

**The growing voice in horror
and speculative fiction.**

Find us at www.maydecemberpublications.com
Or
Email us at contact@maydecemberpublications.com

TW Brown is the author of the **Zomblog** series, his horror comedy romp, ***That Ghoul Ava***, and, of course, the **DEAD** series. Safely tucked away in the beautiful Pacific Northwest, he moves away from his desk only at the urging of his Border Collie, Aoife. (Pronounced Eye-fa)

He plays a little guitar on the side...just for fun...and makes up any excuse to either go trail hiking or strolling along his favorite place...Cannon Beach. He answers all his emails sent to twbrown.maydecpub @gmail.com and tries to thank everybody personally when they take the time to leave a review of one of his works.

His blog can be found at:http://twbrown.blogspot.com

The best way to find everything he has out is to start at his Author Page:

You can follow him on twitter @maydecpub and on Facebook under Todd Brown, Author TW Brown, and also under May December Publications.